Rebel

REBEL

Short Stories from Nepal

compiled & edited by

RAM C. KHATRI

Praise for Rebel

An excellent collection of stories of the recent conflict in Nepal. Written from Maoist and non-Maoist perspectives. They portray the trauma experienced by Nepali people caught up in the vortex of war and represent the social problems of post-war period in a succinct manner.

Dr. Sanjeev Uprety

Selection of the finest stories ever written in Nepali literature about the bitter experiences of the decade-long conflict. I found Mr. Khatri's translation doing justice to the original text.

Bairagi Kainla,

This eclectic collection of short stories is unique and different from others.

Sarubinda

This book reflects the generalization of the conflict and appeals us to develop an approach towards the social movement. Mr. Khatri's enthusiasm to render this outlook into a wider readership is a glory for Nepali literature.

Dr. Govinda P. Sharma (Sukum)

Contents

If we don't end war, war will end us

— **H.G. Wells**

Rebel is a collection of short stories in Nepali literature. It is the English translation of **Vidrohi** carried out by compiler Ram Chandra Khatri.

The collection has altogether 15 short stories written and published recently. The writers range from Manu Brajaki (1942) to Saral Sahayatri (1981). They are all still living and actively writing today. These stories are the reflections of the ten years of conflict and war that came to a close just a few years ago. Nepal has produced a large body of literature recording a decade of horrors.

The same truth of the historical facts of conflict, war, and society ravaged by insurgencies is observed from different facets. Mainly, there are three types of expressions–firstly, those who resist all sorts of wars; secondly, those who support all sorts of devastations for the sake of restructuring; and thirdly, those who are unable to say anything–which meekly undergo suffering or escape it and ignore it.

Nepali literature has recorded the decade-long experiences vividly in different forms of art. Nothing reflects these events so powerfully as art, not even history. They have written the best of novels and short stories, the best of poems and epics, travels, memoires and many more all bearing the impression. Every writer who survived those days has unfailingly created something. The horror is still haunting, the excitement still exhilarating. The experiences of those days are still haunting the memories of many in their psyche like the deep structures of Noam Chomsky. Some people hail it as the great success of the Maoists' 'Great Revolution', while others recorded it as government efforts to do away with armed insurgents that stood against the establishment. All these stories are the results of close and deep observation of the ultimate record of the cruelties of one side or the other. Each story claims for justice and peace from a humanitarian point of view.

There are stronger reasons in favor of revolution for restructuring.

No war is fair. No conflicting situation does justice to humanity. These stand for reconstruction though at the cost of destruction and devastation.

The present decade has witnessed an incomparable degree of progress in Nepali short stories. Various forces have come into play through short stories– collection of stories on themes of love, of sex, of region, of language family, of age group, of gender, etc. have been edited and produced. But the stories based on war and conflict constitute the highest number.

The present decade has been the most remarkable for the production/publication of short stories. Most of them are related to the ten years' experience of war and conflict. Among such collections of stories of this period are: **Stories of Conflict and War and Contemporary Nepali War Stories.** These are exclusively war stories. However, each and every collection produced during this period has stories that remind us of the conflict and war. Whether it is Padmavati Singh's *The Silence of Violence,* Anamol Mani's *Nilima and Deep Darkness,* Bhagirathi Shrestha's *Underground,* Sharmila Khadka's *On the Canvas of Time,* Parashu Pradhan's *Sitas,* Narayan Dhakal's *Aatmahanta,* or the five volumes of short stories Byakul Pathak has edited.

Most of the collections have one or more experiences drawn from the conflicting situations: innocent people being victimized by the war between life and death; being compelled to wait for their final days, or being compelled by the war to desert their own village, town, or being forced to join the armed forces.

Rebel is one of such collection of short stories. It contains 15 short stories, each by a different writer. They include names from famed writers to freshly established young talent. They include those who have observed and interpreted the 'People's Revolution' differently.

The central theme of each story is *fear*. Some of the characters are ready to kill and be killed fearlessly while the others are worried days and night to save their life. Wherever one goes, in the newspapers or in rumors, in sights and scene, the atmosphere and aura, wherever it is, is filled with insecurity, uncertainty, and fear. This psychological fear, doubt, suspicion, and many more have covered the stories in this collection.

Manu Brajaki's *Now, Your Turn, My Dear!* expresses fear psychosis—a real or phantom presence of a Maoist guerilla, or someone in disguise. Fear spreads its net everywhere so a protagonist is in oblivion, or compelled and forced to go somewhere. His heart is torn asunder and is so scared that inwardly he is sure of his death and is almost dead before he faces the real situation. All the members in his family are helpless, nobody has the courage to speak for him or to try to save him or stop him from obeying the call from a dark place. Two or three hours of extreme fear, feeling of hopelessness is enough to kill him. Thus psychological fear has destroyed people, the imaginary being more horrible than reality.

Likewise, the picture of a government office quarter (a frequent target of attack for the rebels) has been presented in Bhaupanthi's *The Senseless Killing of a Man.* The helplessness of the officers or employees, the innocent office bearers, and the great fear they undergo is really dreadful. The rebels toughened by their training and order or teachings are ready to perform any kind of cruelest deed without mercy, love, and humanity. They are shown the utopian dream and are encouraged to carry out sacrifice for the revolution.

Almost all the stories are written against the background given in Maya Thakuri's *The Descending Mountain*. Whatever Ramlal Baje speaks in a loud voice standing on the *Chautara* are the calamities the war brought with it—the bondage between men has ended because everyone predicts his own last hour awaiting.

There is no time for man to study and think, to observe and reason, or wait and rethink. He is in the rage of revolution. They have done unwise and foolish deeds, they have incurred losses irreparable. In the present story Maya Thakuri has presented this very terror in such a way that no reason can control, no word can give people assurance of their survival.

Everything is within that fear circle. Most of the accidents occur due to man's actions, while performing duties and orders; humanity has been left behind. The rebel who shot his own uncle on his office chair and the army personnel who shot Hareram's mother on the riverbank both are sans humanity. They have lost all sensitivity to their fellow men's death.

In this way violence is deeply rooted in the heart of the 'patriot' and 'dutiful', both, whether it be in Khagendra Sangraula's *Hareram's Mother* or Padmavati Singh's *The Silence of Violence*, humanity has disappeared due to violence. Violence is the main theme in this short story.

Most of the victims are innocent. They are tortured, bearing an intolerable, inhuman trauma. Most of them have fear of the abductions, disappearance, and charges, accusation and unpredictable allegations—some are in the mouth of death, others are buried alive, some have suffered mentally, most physically. Like Bam Bahadur, many have lost mental balance, mostly women and children have been severely victimized. There are Chetman's wife and Hareram's mother, Nirmaya, Bishnumaya, Ramaniya, Lakhkhidevi and so on.

Doubt has engulfed everyone. Even the atmosphere is filled with it. They are shocked at the telephone rings, dread talking to their friends; they flee their home, and bid their last goodbye and take their leave, fearing any action from their foes. What a dreadful picture! Fear has filled the town and village, the cave, mountain slope, jungles, and riverbanks—once engulfed by fear, man is so helpless and unprotected.

The character in *Now, Your Turn, My Dear!* is charged with accumulating large sum of wealth or of exploiting people through any pretext (of social service). The character in *The Senseless Killing of a Man* happens to be a victim, an honest government employee. In *Execution*, Bhashkar startles even when the telephone rings. *Our names are also on their hit list*, he hears. How easily do they pass judgment on one's life without allowing any chance for clarification, justification, and appeal!

Who is the agent that takes decision on someone else's life? It's a total chaos. Who holds the key to your life? Horror engulfs everything—it is in the air, in light, atmosphere, land, earth, water and sky. In different forms, there is a gun in front of you, against you. Who is responsible for this horror and death? These stories have such men in different forms.

Bhashkar tries to run away to a safe place seeking protection. Rukmana and her daughter reach a cavern, but violence is awaiting them there too; death is lurking behind you wherever you go. Bhashkar reasons for his self-protection: "If we are in the rebels' bad book despite our constructive work, the objective of the People's War cannot be just and good nor will it end well. This is nothing but a demonic form of terrorism."

But all human reasoning have disappeared from one's heart—only barbarism and cruelty are left. Bhashkar is murdered most cruelly. What a great power, courage and skill was required of Bhagirathi to write such a story, how she could portray the most dreadful moment in one's life! One's hairs stand up to read this story.

Cruelty is practiced from both sides, really from all sides. There are rebels and government armies, there are spies, and looters, gangsters, and fake army, police, even Maoists that take advantage of this chaotic situation. The rebels with the help of the guns tried to achieve their goals; the army, police and spies did this. In fact, both the rebels and the army personnel are just gunmen awaiting orders without logic.

The true operators on both sides are different. They symbolize two types of dictators whose education, training, and operation caused such destruction and brought untold suffering. Neither side stood victorious. Everyone was in doubt and suspicion, in jealousy and rage—as the war wildly raged on, it mindlessly aimed at innocent people by soldiers who were just carrying out order. People could not imagine peace and order being restored. Haiti, Burundi, Timor, Sri Lanka, Afghanistan—many countries of the world saw the dance of death brought out by weapons. Ultimately, the macabre specter descended in our own garden too.

In Ganashyam Dhakal's *Remorse*, there is a picture of a policeman as seen in the eyes of the rebels. The process of cruelty, operation, inhuman treatment of the innocent resulting in rape— it's a dreadful picture. In fact, any side may play this game protected by power, it is similar, whichever side it may be. Only the agent, player or the doer is different yet, the process is same. Dhakal's style is perfectly artistic; he has fully exploited the fear psychosis against a background of reality. Brutal killing has defiled the pure, sacred earth.

In the same way, Mahesh Bikram Shaha's *Buddha in the Slaughterhouse* is a story of great power ending in the enlightenment of a slaughterer. It is one of his best creations included in his **The Son of a Guerilla**, a collection of very powerful, vivid war stories. He is a most successful writer gifted with rare insight and power of words to portray the results of war and conflict very closely.

He has unfailingly and most skillfully painted this psychology in short stories. He penetrates deep into human psychology. He has shown a climax of cruelty and barbarism—how violence has brought about a situation of genocide. At the very symbol of slaughterhouse, when men are slaughtered by a hired man are decapitated, ultimately the butcher's heart changes. He hears the echoes of Buddha. Thus Shah has utilized fantasy exclusively, like Manu Brajaki did in his *Now, Your Turn, My Dear!* This has given a great height to the work of art, though its theme was to show unimaginable cruelty and horror, which led to a change in a hangman's heart.

Among the fifteen, four are women writers. They are Bhagirathi Shrestha, Padmavati Singh, Maya Thakuri, and Sharmila Khadka. The young generation writer Sharmila is very successful in her *Sukanya Alias Nilima*.

In most of the stories, the main actors are male characters involved in violence, threat acts of prosecution, killing and being killed, too. The oppressors are almost all male characters. Unlike this trend, in Sharmila's story, the female character (a young girl) is involved in revolution, she turns out to be a rebel and the situation pictures a moment of battlefield or Maoists' 'operation,' where the district headquarters are destroyed.

The story by Sharmila reveals another facet of truth—why the young people especially were attracted towards Maoist War and why they joined the armed revolution. Everyone has a psychology. There are many reasons to go against the old existing system of governance. This story shows how a young girl was ignored and how administration has created an absurd situation. This is the story of a young warrior who believes Maoist War will solve her problems and create a just society.

In the same way, Roshan Thapa 'Neerav' in *Unbearable* presents a picture of horror and barbarism; without a mention of specific time and place (in the style of science fiction), though this may be extended to any place and time.

The author has adopted a more indirect and symbolic technique. When a character returns home after 12 years, he sees a corpse lying completely naked by the road—it was his sister's, with her breast cut in a public place. Another corpse was in a similar situation of his own beloved. This style clearly depicts how barbarous those days had been—especially the violence against women was dreadful. This is the result of barbarism that war brought to man. Then the hero promises to stand against such barbarism and the protection of women.

Rajkumar Dikpal's *Liwang-2006* is also a great symbolic picture of a war front that has destroyed many lives. Dilsara is found seated all the time on a ground of the headquarters with her eyes fixed to the wild western mountain. She has lost mental balance since she lost her son in the battle. She is overwhelmed with grief and keeps looking towards high Gwarpa Mountain, lying far away where her son had disappeared.

Like an insane person, she spends the days staring at the hill. It is the mothers who suffered the pangs of conflict and war most of all. They lost their love ones and they became helpless. Dilsara and Hareram's mother are similar mother figures in that are suffering in a similar way. What a great art has been used to portray those moments of grief! These mothers who suffered such traumatic moments are still waiting for their lost ones.

The Shadow of Gun shows a change of heart. A rebel becomes different in Homshankar's story. The intention of a warmonger is open by a wielding gun only they have accumulated power and wealth, while the gun has destroyed values and civilization itself. Ultimately, what is the value of this sacrifice? The war has gripped distant villages, weapon and ammunition have terrorized all, innocent animals and people have lost their lives for no reason. The character sees reason in the end and concludes that the cause of our tragedy is gun, the power controlled by gun. What happens if you throw away the gun? How helpless does a person become? He would like to get rid of the gun, even its shadow, the first cause of brutality and ruin.

Nirmal Acharaya has used a journalistic style in his *A Civil Servant's Diary*. This is the monologue of a soldier that shows the cruelty and madness of a commander as well as how ammunition and war weapons are misused during critically chaotic days.

The last story is Saral Sahayatri's *We, Two Soldiers*. The writer has compared the lives of two kinds of soldiers—the rebel and the army. Each has a specific ambition. The Maoist promise to make a village free from injustice, exploitation, and their poverty and ignorance; whereas the government army promises to protect a nation—its borders and more. Each person has their own logic; those who stand up for what's right.

The world history witnessed innumerable wars and insurgencies and what means of violence were used. The results of these actions have become similar. But truly great uprisings and revolutions like French Revolution, American Revolution, and Russian Revolution have changed the course of human history. The guerilla-style warfare fought during modern times is quite different. Those who actually participate are the humble people but such actions are operated by a limited number of leaders who are ambitious, can convince people and promise them a different kind of future. The leaders mostly have desire for power; the ultimate goal of all lust of wars and insurgencies is power, the rule and their government. Those who fight for them are the humble men, nameless, homeless followers, who cannot think of the result and who are glorified by a false sense of sacrificing for the motherland, not surviving for a peaceful life.

This is one reason why war should be despised—there are reasons in favor of war too.

Thus the present collection is translated beautifully and further edited properly. Mr. Khatri has sincerely done this job. No need to say that his bent for translation is quite deep. He has already brought two works into Nepali, namely **Bishwaka Utkrista Aadhunik Kathaharu** and **Rupantaran**, translations of some American and European short stories and Franz Kafka's **The Metamorphosis**, respectively. He has proved his skill and experience in the translation of the present volume of short stories.

He has thus contributed immensely towards producing the samples of contemporary Nepali short stories to a wide English speaking community. For the lack of translational activities, very few people know about Nepali literature in the world. It is not known even to the neighboring countries of Asia.

Though Nepali has good number of titles in poetry and novels, there are hardly any in short stories. Some titles to appear so far are Stories from Nepal, Selected Stories from Nepal, Begging Bowl and Other Stories, Stories of Conflict and War, Beyond the Frontiers: Women's Stories from Nepal, Buddha and Other Stories, Faulty Glass and Other Stories, among others.

This evidence is enough to justify that Ram Chandra has accomplished a most commendable task so I congratulate him on this remarkable achievement.

Govinda Raj Bhattarai

Professor of English

Tribhuvan University

Kathmandu, Nepal

A Few Words

The stories in this anthology share a unique distinction: all navigate the different aspects of the Maoist insurgency in Nepal when the country was thrown chaotically into war. The stories were originally published in Nepali, and despite the fact that translation of serious literature is challenging, I took the task upon myself to share the pains, sorrows, and effects of the decade-long conflict with the world.

My daily confrontation with news related to the war, and the turbulent situation of the country while I was associated with *The Himalayan Times,* sparked my interest in translating these stories about conflict. I wanted to delve into the realities of the war in ways the news did not. In fact, this collection is the outcome of my research on war and conflict, and of a lengthy process I went through. I visited a number of areas ravaged by the war, a number of injured victims and listened to their painful tales as a journalist before I selected these specific stories. I studied some 200 short stories written on the Maoist War by Nepali writers and the same number of stories by American and European writers in an attempt to know the rhetoric and language used in short stories. I also consulted the writers, took their views regarding the contents of their war stories, and finally selected these stories, which represent the real scenario of the decade-long conflict. Regarding the length of these stories, each is not more than 4,000 words. I reviewed my translation multiple times. It took me three years to compile, translate, and edit the stories. These stories examine the various devastating aspects of the conflict.

Manu Brajaki's *Now, Your Turn, My Dear!* offers an

intimate look at the crippling fear and tragedy that befall a couple, while Bhaupanthi's *The Senseless Killing of a Man* focuses on the gratuitous killing of a government officer. Maya Thakuri's *The Descending Mountain* explores the grim reality of rural life during the conflict, and Padmavati Singh's *The Silence of Violence* centers on the plight of a displaced village woman. Bhagirathi Shrestha's *Execution* mingles the disturbed mental state and execution of its main character with the questionable war-time values of society. Sharmila Khadka's *Sukanya, Alias Nilima* presents an injured officer's stream of consciousness during his hazy awakening after an attack, and Roshan Thapa's *Unbearable* follows a man's emotional return to his razed village. In Khagendra Sangraula's *Hareram's Mother,* we suffer through an old woman's lamentation over the death of her son. Similarly, we endure the plight of a poor farmer in Ghanashyam Dhakal's *Remorse.* In both Homshankar Bastola's *The Shadow of a Gun* and Saral Sahayatri's *We, Two Soldiers* we are presented with both sides of the war and its destructive ability to divide close friends. Mahesh Bikram Shah's *Buddha in the Slaughterhouse* presents an eerie scene of death and depravity, reminiscent of Hitler's concentration camps. A young soldier observes a pregnant woman's murder in Nirmal Acharya's *A Civil Servant's Diary,* while Rajkumar Dikpal's *Liwang, 2006* tells the harrowing tale of an old woman. Finally, we accompany a captive soldier on his march to death in Nawa Silwal's *The Prisoner.*

I have tried my best to convey the subtle nuances of the Nepali source text in my translation, accepting the fact that translation by nature must involve loss and gain. I have attempted to preserve either the literal image of the source text or its essence when preserving both is impossible.

My dream of preparing this book in this form would not have materialized if I had not gotten the support, advice, and cooperation of several people. I would like to express my sheartfelt thanks to the writers for giving me permission to compile, translate, and publish their stories. I express my sincere thanks to Dr. Govinda Raj Bhattarai for recognizing my work and writing the critical introduction of this book. Moreover, his inspiring guidelines have been fruitful since the beginning of my career as a literary translator.

A lion's share of my thanks goes to Kate Saunders who seriously and sensitively proofread each of the stories. Similarly, I would like to thank Tek Narayan Dhakal and Rachel Slaiman for checking and double-checking my translation, and Bal Ram Adhikari for his positive feedback.

I am indebted to Dr. Sanjeev Uprety, Bairagi Kainla, Manjushree Thapa, Sarubinda, and Sukum Sharma for their critical and thoughtful blurbs for this book. I am also grateful to poetess and essayist Momila for helping me to reach some of the writers. I would also like to thank Hira, my better-half, for her patience and encouragement throughout this process.

Ram C. Khatri

New York, USA

MANUBRAJAKI (1942)

Born in Aurahi VDC of Mahottari district in the central Terai of Nepal, Chetman Singh Bhandari is popularly known as Manu Brajaki in Nepali literature. His first story was published when he was twenty. His collections of short stories include *Abamulyan* (Devaluation, 1981), *Timri Swasni Ra Ma* (Your Wife and Me, 1989), *Bhabisya Yatra* (Journey towards the Future, 1995), *Paradarshi Manchhe* (A Transparent Person, 2004), and *Aamalai Bechnu Hudaina, Lata* (You Fool, Don't Sell Your Mother, under publication). A leading short story writer, Brajaki was awarded the Sajha Prize for his second collection *Timri Swasni Ra Ma* and the Manuscript Prize for *Bhabisya Yatra*.

Brajaki skillfully presents a slice of life and critically examines the absurdities underlying the individual, society, and social events in his stories. "I give top priority to presenting the whole of life out of a small social setting, a particular character and specific event in my stories," he says. According to Dr. Laxman Prasad Gautam, Manu Brajaki can weave "extraordinary stories" from commonplace social events and social issues. The present story, *Aba Timro Palo Ho!* (Now, Your Turn, My Dear!), appeared while the decade-long conflict between the Maoists and the government of Nepal reached its boiling point. The story offers a close view of the blinding fear and tragedy that befalls a couple.

Now, Your Turn, My Dear!

"Don't leave for the jungle," she pleaded.

I looked at my wife's mournful eyes, which were filled with sympathy. They were saying even more.

They were saying, "Please don't go. I'd rather die together with you."

They were saying, "How shall I live alone, taking on the burden of our children?" They were saying, "Why do you go alone? Didn't we exchange vows to live and die for each other?"

Of course, we married promising to live and die for each other. How easy it would have been to leave home if the institution called "family"—that bond between a husband and wife—did not exist in present society. How easy it would be for me to leave the family. Neither her *sindoor* nor *tilhari* would allow me from leaving home.

I knew the meaning of my wife's mournful eyes—we should live and die for each other. Also I knew that one has to die for others to live. One can live here only after the death of someone else.

"Now, it's my turn."

As I muttered these words, she pleaded more somberly, "Please, don't say so. Don't say it!"

"They have prepared a list. We are in a queue," I said to her.

I saw her eyes sinking to hollowness. They looked blind. Never in my life had I thought that one day I should have to see my beloved's eyes in such a state. All this was due to my "turn" today.

I left the courtyard and entered my room to get dressed.

My eyes focused on the photos fixed to the wall on the right shelf. There were three photos adorned with *achheta* and flowers. In the center was a photo of Lord Buddha, the apostle of peace, non-violence, and justice. To the left was the righteous Lord Ram, the slayer of Ravan.

To the right was Lord Krishna, the destroyer of Kauravs. Ram had a bow and Krishna had his circular weapon, the *sudarshan chakra*. Both mighty lords love to fight evildoers and their duty is to kill them. For the winners, the defeated rivals are always seen as sinners or wicked.

I had thought of removing the photos, except the one of weaponless Buddha, but I let the latter remain between the bow-bearer and the chakra-holder as my wife prayed to them all.

"Did I mock the present world?" I asked myself.

Instantly, I remembered Lord Buddha in the land of his birthplace when the country brimmed with murder and violence.

I was frustrated with making "donations" and receiving threats; I was also tired of explaining myself.

Did I commit a crime by getting involved in social service?

I could not find my clothes because I was thinking fitfully.

"Today is my turn."

"I have to go to the jungle today."

"I have been called for today."

As I repeated these words, I hopelessly turned my eyes from the shelf on the wall and shouted in a frantic voice, "Oh Radha! Radha! Come upstairs for a while. I can't find my clothes to get changed. They were right here, hanging on the nail."

"I put your clothes under your pillow after washing and folding them," Radha spoke from the porch instead of coming upstairs and showing me the clothes.

"Oh, why does she have such a voice?" I wondered. "She must be speaking alone from the porch, hanging her head in dejection."

"Is this a time to sit with your head bent?" I shouted. "I'm telling you to come upstairs. I need to change my clothes."

Though Radha had already told me where the clothes were, I wanted to see her before I left for the jungle. I wanted her alone in the room so that I could say something to her. The children were reading books on the porch below.

She entered the room, covering her face with the corner of her sari. I noticed that she was emotional. "I beg you, don't go! Why do you need your clothes? There's no need to change your clothes," she said nervously, moved by love.

"Oh, you're right. Why should I change? I'm not going to any wedding party, feast, or festival. I'm not going to any market either. In fact, I'm going to the jungle."

I looked at the clothes I was wearing.

I was in a dirty white T-shirt, torn at the collar, and threadbare black pants with torn knees. Such clothes were good enough to go to the jungle. Radha was right, I did not need to change my clothes.

"Who the hell came to call for me? Tell me," I asked her directly, forgetting about the clothes.

"I don't know him . . . a fourteen- or fifteen-year-old boy . . . wearing a red T-shirt and . . . while going to the teashop . . . ,"

Radha gasped, her body shaking as she wept.

"You little fool, why are you crying like this? Since I am a social worker, they might have called me to inquire about or discuss some issue. Don't cry."

No matter how much I controlled myself to console her, I was crying within.

Hearing my coaxing *don't cry,* she could not help weeping and let the tears roll from her eyes like a broken dam.

As I wrapped my arms around her and caressed her head, face, and neck, I noticed that there was no *tilhari* around her neck, no bangles on her wrist. She had no earrings either. Those jewelries of married Hindu women had been taken off her ears, neck, and wrist three months ago. She looked like a widow prior to my death.

Radha, my darling, a woman of great heart!

****

Yes, three months ago, shortly after midnight, a misfortune fell upon us. Somebody kicked at the door of our thatch-roofed house. I was awake at the time. I was reading or writing something. I don't remember whether it was for the school or my adult education program. That blow had almost broken the door. From the yard below, we heard an order loud enough to deafen our ears.

"Hey, hypocrite social worker, Get down here!"

I looked out of the window and saw ten or eleven people with weapons in the moon-blanched night. Then I turned my head to look at the neighbors' houses, which had sunk into a dead silence. Nobody came out. Hearing the racket, they holed up in their houses. The neighborhood deliberately slumbered like a graveyard.

Before this as well, I had received three warning letters addressed to "the hypocrite social worker." In those letters were stringent orders for me to discontinue my social service. We were probably on their black list because I disobeyed their letters.

As the holder of a School Leaving Certificate, I had chosen to become involved in social service. Politics was not my interest. I did not have the slightest inclination towards any of the political parties such as the Congress, the Communist, the Rastriya Prajatantra, or the Sadbhabana. How could I be a hypocrite when I had been benevolently engaging in social service? How come I was a hypocrite when the people applauded me for my social service?

But at that time there was no way of explaining all these things.

After the group of rebels had descended on our home and ordered me into the yard, Radha and the children woke up. The frightened children bunched together in the bed and started to weep.

I had no choice but to go to the yard. The rebels greeted me with two kicks after seeing Radha coming after me, petrified. "Hypocrite! You're still continuing with social service, eh? Now, pay this fine!" they said.

One of them standing with a weapon helped me up, as I was lying on the ground after I had received the second kick. The next one pointed his torchlight towards me. I saw a pamphlet placed in my hand. It requested five thousand rupees. Immediately, I sensed that it was an order, not a request.

"Bring the money at once!"

I entered the house without a word. Radha, joining her hands in front of them, was shaking like a leaf.

I took out of the cupboard one thousand rupees, which I had kept to buy clothes for our eldest daughter, and fifteen hundred rupees, which I had collected for my adult education program. I placed the twenty-five hundred rupees in the leader's hands.

Seeing only half of their demand, they gave two more kicks. I fell on the ground and could not rise immediately. As I got up with my hands on my waist, I saw Radha standing with her jewelry in her hands. Those were the ornaments that symbolized her husband was living. She wanted to say something. She spread her hands before the leader of the group. The leader seemed confused whether to take the jewelry from her or not. However, another armed person next to him seized it.

"It's OK! Let's go. From now on, if you repeat the dishonest work, you will face severe consequences."

After they had left, I embraced my wife. I was stunned. "You are great, Radha. No woman gives away her prized jewelry so readily," I said.

"My fortune. My life. It's you!" said Radha, trembling.

Then in the neighboring houses, lights were turned on, doors were opened, and the neighbors appeared at my yard asking, "What happened, sir? What's the matter?"

****

I had, thus, a fresh memory of three months before. I was greatly moved by seeing Radha crying with her empty neck and ears.

Even after the incident I had not given up participating in the adult education program and other community work. Because of this, though, I might have been called to the jungle today.

Radha was weeping inwardly, stuffing the corner of her sari into her mouth. She did not want her children reading on the porch below to hear their mother weeping.

No matter how much my heart and mind were debilitated, it was my burden to go to the place I was called. "Where did they tell me to go, Radha?" I asked.

Radha, with her terror-stricken eyes, stared at me. Her eyes were making the same request, "Please, don't go. It's your turn now." She spoke under her breath, "To the meadow where the spring near the Mahadev Temple is located. They have asked you to get there by noon."

I looked at my wristwatch. Ten o'clock already. The jungle can be reached after walking two kilometers along the paddy field. A small meadow with a spring appears after walking for a few minutes from the edge of the jungle. In one corner of the meadow is the Mahadev Temple, which is attached to a hill. For many years a yogi lived there in a hut, but he vanished due to the insecurity and nobody knows when. Local people would sometimes go there for a picnic.

Facing towards the wall and holding her mouth, Radha was still crying, her body shrugged with fear.

I came out of the room with the clothes I was wearing, reached the ladder and, wearing my worn-out Hawaiian slippers, I said in a faint voice, "Now I'll go."

Radha followed me up to the door and urged, "Please, don't go. Now it's your turn." After a short pause, she spoke in a voice fainter than mine, "Have a meal before you go."

"A meal!" my voice trailed off.

I silently climbed down the ladder, and making a round of the holy *tulasi* plant in our yard and the *lalupate* flowers at the gate. I came to the narrow path bordered with bushes on both sides and then I made a dash for the meeting place.

Even at the moment of tearful parting I could not bring myself to look in my wife's eyes because I would find them making the same request, "Please, don't go. Now it's your turn."

Before this, three people from our area had gone into the jungle. Two of them were found dead in a ghastly condition while the third person's whereabouts were still unknown.

While walking all the way from the village, the people I met sounded like they were making the same request, "Please sir, don't go. Now it's your turn." But in fact they were simply asking, "Where are you going, sir?"

I feared for what was to come as I walked up to the paddy field having lost consciousness. I was lost in the memory of Radha, my children, my village, my country, and so forth.

I am unable to narrate hereafter. I've told my story up to here. Now, listen to the fearsome and horrified state of my heart from Manu Brajaki —

According to Manu Brajaki —

Chetman Sir, the social worker of this area, was staggering on his feet. Even the slippers he wore had stopped making a sound. He walked amidst the green paddy field as if he was a dry leaf flying in a storm of horror.

The social worker, age forty, lower middle class and a patient of high blood pressure, had forgotten to have his meal and medicine before leaving home. While faltering on the field, he thought, "What shall be my punishment—splintered bamboo, sticks, or bullets?" A vision of his own grisly murder came to him, and he was extremely agitated by an intense memory of his family, which was going to be left in lurch without him.

–Remembering his wife, Radha, his legs trembled.

–Remembering his eldest daughter, Uma, his body shivered.

–Remembering his second daughter, Shanta, his heart beat fast.

–With the memory of his little son, he was unable to think clearly.

–His whole existence was dismantled with the memory of his society and country.

Walking across the field, he reached the edge of the jungle. A few cattle were grazing there. A little ahead, shepherds were playing a game of *khopi*. They stopped playing and stared at Chetman Sir. He raised his head to look at them. Today he could not tell the boys, "Little ones, don't play *khopi*, you should read." He felt as if they were glaring at him and saying —

"Go, old man, go. It's your turn now!"

He felt a growing heaviness on the left side of his shoulder and ribcage. His eyes filmed over. His back hunched more. His heart pounded faster.

Only a few minutes passed by, but the distance seemed so far away. While he was staggering and stooping through a narrow track bordered with *dhurseli* and *banmara* weed, he saw a boy of around fifteen in a red T-shirt. He was coming towards Chetman Sir.

The boy suddenly turned back and shouted.

"Look! Look! Sir has arrived."

Hearing him, Chetman Sir's staggering legs shook at the knees with his back stooped, and his heart sank deeper. His fear escalated.

He stood still and began to look around with blurred eyes.

A moment later, five to seven men appeared from out of the bush behind the boy. They spoke in a chorus:

"Come sir, come! Welcome to our picnic. We sent this boy to your house to call you without mentioning the picnic so that we might surprise you. Please forgive us for that."

As they approached, Chetman Sir recognized them — they were his friends from the neighboring village. Because of the sudden happiness he felt, his blood surged through his whole body. He felt his chest exploding with each heartbeat. His bent body stretched out. Then, pressing his chest tightly with his right hand, he fell to the ground, face down.

"Sir, sir what happened to you? What's the problem, Sir!" the friends ran towards him as he collapsed.

Thus Chetman freed himself forever from the fear, fright, and terror of this life.

And his Radha became a widow.

*****

BHAUPANTHI (1944)

Bhaupanthi was born Tilak Prasad Sharma in Gulmi district, western Nepal. A successful short-story writer, novelist, and poet, he published his first story, entitled *Rangahin* (Colorless), in 1965. His first published book was *Palans* (Flame of the Forest, 1972), a novella. His short story collections include *Euta Aakarko Barema* (About a Shape, 1975), *Sambandha* (Connection, 1979), *Sattachyut Ra Aru Kathaharu* (Dethroned and Other Stories, 1996), *Sanakhat Ra Aru Kathaharu* (Identification and Other Stories, 2010), and *Ishwar Pani Sutchha, Nadi Pani Nidaunchha* (God Also Sleeps, River Also Slumbers, 2007). Bhaupanthi, the first litterateur to receive the Mainali Story Prize (1981), was honored with the *Rastriya Pratibha Puraskar* and other accolades.

In his stories, Bhaupanthi gives top priority to the events taking place in the country and to the "bitter human experiences and terror" that burden innocent people. Regarding his story writing, Roshan Thapa 'Neerav' observes: "With his craft, Bhaupanthi powerfully presents the various events taking place in the country and the events befalling its people." Taken from his collection *Sanakhat Ra Aru Kathaharu,* the present story, *Euta Manchhe Phosama* (The Senseless Killing of a Man), focuses on the senseless killing of a government officer before the backdrop of a conflict-hit Nepal, when the country was teeming with corruption, murder, violence, and abduction.

The Senseless Killing of a Man

"He was not willing to go to the office today," said the officer's widow in her first reaction to the incident. It seemed that the officer had had a premonition of his imminent murder. Other members of his family expressed their ignorance, however.

The fact that the dead man was not in the mood to go to his office was not enough evidence for an investigation into his death. It was only evidence that a man can do nothing once death begins to drag him. This was how people all across the country were killed. The officer's death taught people that man can do nothing to prevent death. It was a sinister time when people were being killed and the existence of an institution, known as the government, had not only grown feeble, but its importance had faded completely.

"Dear, if you don't want to, don't go to the office today," his wife had said to him before he left for work in his official car that morning. She was worried that her husband was bearing the burdens of the country's responsibilities and that the burden was debilitating him. She had, however, not verbalized her feelings.

The officer went to the office that morning. He had a heavy heart not because he had a premonition of his death, but because he had witnessed countless cases of murder and violence and they made him feel insecure. He looked a bit unhappy. The reason could have been some problems in his family or something else. For him, going to the office was akin to being tethered like an animal.

Office workers are accustomed to going to their respective offices, a habit that eventually turns into a life-long routine. Like domesticated animals that return to their shelter to be tethered by their necks or legs after grazing all day. They must also prepare themselves physically and mentally for returning to their offices the following morning. Though service seekers rush to catch them, they rarely find office workers in their chairs when they need them. Despite public wrath, these employees do not improve, like thieving animals that secretly enter a cultivated field.

The dead man was an officer, not an ordinary employee, but a boss! He was an honest officer, the kind that can rarely be found in government offices, who makes his living on a government salary. The importance of an honest officer like him might be insignificant among those who are corrupt, but this officer had preserved with pride the reputation that honest employees like him could also be found in government offices.

After his promotion, a new nameplate was put on the door of his office. He was elated to see his name on it. He was equally happy to be transferred to the new office and was grateful to the government. However, his joy soon fizzled. Upon learning that the district he was posted to have been affected by rebels, he started looking at people doubtfully. He did not believe that the headquarters were within the circle of security. Recently, a branch office of the Agricultural Development Bank had been blown up with a pressure-cooker bomb.

The Land Revenue Office and the Municipal Office were also destroyed after he took command of his new post. He thought that the rebels had cowardly detonated the bombs to threaten him. People said that the rebels planned to capture the city. First they would seek shelter around the neighboring districts and then they would attack.

While going to and returning from his office, he saw the marketplaces submerged in a silence, fear of the rebel's attack seemed to be floating in the air. People talked and laughed very little. They were not carrying out their daily chores. Only a few people could be seen in the markets with little to no activity after five or six in the evening. Their inactivity bred terror.

The nameplate read "OUT" when the officer entered his office on the day he was to die. His eyes were fixed on the nameplate—a final glimpse before his death. Sometimes he would replace "OUT" with "IN" himself by sliding the plate's wooden pane. The importance of officers like him was dwindling. The lawlessness of an organized group was looming large around the office premises. Though he realized this fact with a heavy heart, he had begun to pretend that he was unaware of what was truly happening.

He would be careful not to show his internal feelings of disagreement with the junior employees, thinking that in such situations they might spy on him. Later, it was known that he himself began to slide the wooden pane of his nameplate to "IN" when entering his office and to "OUT" while leaving for home, rather than having a peon do it for him because otherwise the peons would possibly protest. This is how he retained his post, which had turned out to be one of mockery, insult, and cowardice. His mind filled with the fear of any possible destructive acts in his office.

Each morning, the man would be in a rush to reach his office on time. He was conscious of punctuality though he was the chief, an ideal chief! He derived no personal benefit from his regularity. In other offices, there were hardly any officers who reached their office on time. In their opinions, those who maintained punctuality were not qualified to be an officer. They thought that officers should have unique dignity, manner, persistence, and personal view, just as the whorl of a fingerprint was unique. These characteristics establish the identity of the officers among their service seekers and office staff. But what did you say to the officer who reaches his office at the right time and opens his own door like a peon? Such a feeble and dimwitted officer is a little better than one that is dead. However, this officer was indifferent to such thinking.

That day, the officer forgot to slide his nameplate's wooden pane to "IN" after he had entered it. The reason could have been his forgetfulness, a sickness, or something else. Later, after his death, his office doorkeeper said, "Our boss had to leave the world forever, that's why he left "OUT" on his nameplate. These words could have been a true homage to the death of his boss, or mere irony.

The office had been opened as usual yet, the employees had yet to arrive. The people around were not unaware that office work did not start until all the employees came, settled themselves in their chairs, smoked one or two cigarettes, and gossiped for more than half an hour. The peon was not yet standing guard at the officer's door and the office had no trained security.

Meanwhile, three young men entered the office. One had a black bag while another halted behind his friends under the pretext of lighting a cigarette while the other two went in. The young man at the door had a pistol, so did the others who had entered. Nobody noticed. One of the two men carefully took out his pistol and waylaid the peon, who was climbing down the stairs to begin his duty. The peon had heard of such incidents, and now he was going to witness one. His friends who had faced such situations in their offices had suggested that it was best to remain silent and stay out of the way rather than protest. Execution and punishment are for the upper echelons of bureaucracy; revolutions are for the working class. This idea was circulated among all peons.

The incident was like one that could be read in newspapers or seen on television. The peon soon sensed that the rebels had come to blow up his office building. He was so scared that he almost pissed himself; however, his fear was tempered by the fact that he was accustomed to seeing similar incidents in the news. On the top of that, the peon remembered his friends explaining what should be done when such incidents take place. After the peon had been subdued, the man with the bag climbed the stairs. Later, while the peon was describing the facial features of his boss' murderer, an image flashed into his mind—the man with the bag was somehow like his boss. But he was afraid to explain this to the police. He was sympathetic towards his murdered boss: the officer was not overbearing like other officers; he did not speak in a commanding voice, and he used to carry out official work on his own if the peons and other staff dilly-dallied. He was a simple, dimwitted officer, more like a peon than a boss.

The young man with the bag could not find the right place to put it. He stood confused before the officer's door. He read "OUT" on the nameplate. In one corner of his heart he had no intention of killing men, but it was another matter to destroy government property. The group had begun to receive a number of complaints over the killing of innocent people. There was even growing pressure from the international community against the killing of innocent people. It had explained to the public that it was a revolution in which innocent persons might be killed, but the party high command had already realized that such concepts were not convincing anyone.

The young man, who had gone to the jungle to join the rebels and establish a people's state, read "OUT" on the nameplate and thought that the officer had not yet arrived. This was not a time for the officers to be at work. Such conditions would not have occurred if civil servants had done their works on time. This rationalization struck the young man. He thought it right to place his bag in the room before him. What better place was there to blow up than the chief's office?

The young man was surprised to see a man in the officer's chair as he opened the door. "He must be the officer," the young man thought, "though peons are sometimes found sitting in their boss' chair, pretending to be officers." The unfulfilled wishes of men are expressed in this way. But this man was not like a peon. He was wearing a cap—a new cap. Seeing his wan face, the rebel could not be certain that he was the officer.

"You'd better get out of here. We're planting a bomb," he said boldly. "We're going to destroy the office."

"Who in God's name are you?" asked the man in the chair. "This is no place for a bomb. Why are you doing this?" The man, who was ashen with fear, was indeed an officer. His fear was obvious in his voice. The young man recognized him. Despite his helplessness, his officer's tone seemed arrogant.

The light that entered through the window illuminated the young man's face.

"Who on earth are you?" the officer asked again.

"He is the officer," the young man concluded from his tone.

The officer looked at the young man, trying to remember something. Then a look of recognition spread across his face. "You are Ramesh — my missing nephew, aren't you? Why did you become a guerilla?" the officer exclaimed with an avuncular pride.

The young man was confused at first and then attempted to speak in a normal tone, "Uncle!" His tone was cordial, but bombs and cordiality do not go together. He became conscious of himself. He told himself that a revolution requires sacrifices from a father, uncle, nephew, and son. Such a bold determination towards the party's revolution would set an example. What would it be like if he shot his own uncle? He was angry at society, thinking that it had been gripped by nepotism and favoritism. He wanted to free society from this plague. He was drunk on the wine of revolution, and he was on the verge of becoming a hero.

"What if he is my uncle? After all, he is a greedy landlord." He returned to his earned ruthlessness and said, "This is a revolution. What is an uncle and what is a nephew, sir? We're at the peak of our revolution. It is a high time for the next phase." He placed the bag on the officer's table and quickly walked out.

Hey, hey, why are you doing this? Oh, for heaven's sake take this bag out of here . . . The young man heard his uncle shout as he left the room.

'So, I'm going to be killed by my own nephew . . . ?' The baffled officer did not believe what was happening before his eyes. His urging words were barred by the door, which was latched from the outside. "Any moment the bomb might explode," the young man cried from beyond the door, "Long live our revolution!"

"Long live . . . !"

The young man's voice was filled with a resolute determination. In this way, he took the revolution a step further.

By the time security officials came to investigate the incident, the young man had run off. "Three young men came . . . How could I recognize them? They shouted that a bomb had been planted inside and ran westwards, urging each other to flee," explained the peon.

The news had already reached the officer's family. His wife, with uncontrollable tears, repeated the same words, "He was not willing to go to . . ." Her voice trailed off this time.

Then a mournful howling was heard far and wide.

*****

MAYATHAKURI (1946)

Born in Lucknow, India, Maya Thakuri is a special name in Nepali story writing. Her first short-story collection is *Najureko Jodi* (An Incompatible Couple, 1973). Her other collections of stories include *Gamalako Phool* (Flower in a Vase, 1976), *Sanghu Tarepachhi* (After Crossing the Bridge, 1982), *Maya Thakurika Kathaharu* (The Stories of Maya Thakuri, 1991), and *Aama Januhos* (Please, Go Mother, 2007). She has been honored with the Mainali Story Prize, Ratna Shree Gold Medal, *Rastriya Nari Samman,* and other awards. Apart from writing short stories, she composes songs and poems and one collection of songs, *Indradhanus* (The Rainbow, 2006), has been published.

Maya Thakuri writes her stories using ideal realism and bases them on women's suffering. Her stories raise the call for women's freedom. Regarding her story writing, Ram Prasad Gyawali observes: "One special thing in Maya Thakuri's stories is the depth of sensitivity, the sensational description of pitiable situations or characters, and the presentation of ordinary events." T

he motive of her stories is to make people aware of social evils by helping them realize a "deep human sensitivity." The present story, *Pahad Orlirahechha* (The Descending Mountain), is taken from her collection, *Aama Januhos*. In the story, she depicts rural reality. The story follows a helpless woman living in a rural village with her daughter and son, who all become the victims of social evil.

The Descending Mountain

"Bomb, gun, lethal weapon, explosion, clash, deadly attack, arson, murder, abduction, arrest, torture, violence. Now there is no need to flip through the pages of a dictionary to grasp the underlying meaning of these words. This is because many people from infants to elders are losing their precious lives in the maelstrom of such destructive rage.

"Ultimately, what crime have the children committed when they are simply enjoying their multicolored lives, exposing life's many layers? Why were golden dreams seized from their innocent eyes? For whom and for what reason are they made the victims of violence? Why are our daughters being rendered homeless? Whichever side the killed belonged to, the victim's families have to bear the brunt of the tragedy. Consequently, women and children in particular will have to live with an unbearable load of pain throughout their lives.

"What dreadful maelstrom has our country fallen into? Empathy, feeling, and love are now void.

"The political leaders are shoving each other, competing for power and positions. A sense of insecurity has engulfed the common people.

"People living in the same village and locality have started looking at each other suspiciously.

"They used to say that a good neighbor's duty was to help others in difficulty. Though in today's adverse situation, when one knocks at the door of his neighbor crying for help to protect his life and property, the neighbor shuts himself in so as to save his own life and property.

"The sonorous sounds of conch shells used to be heard at least somewhere in our country, but those melodies have slowly faded away amidst the painful cries of innocent people.

"The fear of war has left the country in a dreadfully silent state. If the situation continues, today's history will be written with blood."

Ramlal Baje, standing at the *chautari*, was speaking at the top of his voice.

He was taking long breaths.

"Baje! Our village is being deserted. Youths have left to go abroad. The children and the elders are also leaving the village. We only see fallow lands wherever we look. The *dhiki* and *janto* have been replaced with newfangled machines. The water is continuously wasting away from the spring. The village has become an inhospitable place to live. No one ever imagined that they would have to see this nightmarish time," Karmabir, the next most senior person of the village, said to Ramlal Baje, blowing out a deep breath.

"Exactly, brother. Seeing the plight of our village, I feel like crying. Our country won't exist if the situation continues," Ramlal Baje spoke with a deep sigh.

At seventy-six, Ramlal Baje had passed two thirds of his life as a schoolteacher in the village. Villagers trusted his words and followed his suggestions. He had been helping them as best he could whenever they were in trouble.

Moreover, he was successful at reviving the hopes of frustrated people with his eloquent speech. But when the whole country began to submerge into violence, terror, and murder, he was agitated from within.

His village was ravaged by war. Huts were blown up with bombs. People were made homeless. Several innocent children, youths, and defenseless elders were shot dead. It seemed that fear dwelled in the villager's eyes and had become deeply rooted in their hearts.

The villagers were forced to open their doors when a group of torchlight holders came for a raid and landed their boots on their doors. Finding themselves threatened at gunpoint, the villagers did not even know the reason for the brutality.

****

For her safety, Rukmana, a terrified mother, had fled her village with her nine-year-old daughter, Muna, to an unknown place. They had been hiding in a narrow jungle cave for the past three days after having walked a whole day from the village.

"Aren't we returning to our village, mother?" Muna had asked, crunching the grains of parched corn and soybean that her mother had brought from home.

"How could we possibly return, daughter! We'd better go away somewhere else," Rukmana said sadly.

"Aren't we taking our brother with us, mother? What would he do if he came home and did not see us?" the innocent girl asked somberly.

"Child, you know your brother hasn't come home for many days. Nobody knows where he is. In the village, a group of people would come by day and night and threaten, 'Where is your son? We'll punish that spy.' Then again another group of people would terrorize me, enquiring, 'Where have you hidden the property he looted? We'll punish him once he is arrested.' But I knew nothing of his condition, dead or alive.

"I pinned my hope on your brother after your father passed

away. I was rearing three souls, working hard from dawn to dusk. He dropped out of school when he was in ninth grade, saying that he preferred to go abroad to earn money. 'Dear son, you ought to study well so that you can earn money in our country,' I tried to persuade him, but my advice fell on deaf ears. He began to badger me into selling land after learning that a huge sum of money is required to go abroad. I was ready to fulfill his demands, even selling the piece of land, but later I came to know that the money from the land would not be sufficient to send him abroad. Then your good-for-nothing brother started visiting the liquor shops with hooligans. Did you not see how he would come home dead drunk and start quarrelling with me about everything? I tried to persuade him many times to stop, but all my efforts fell flat."

"I showed your brother's horoscope to an astrologer, and he said that his bad behavior was because of poorly aligned stars. The astrologer advised me to arrange a *swastishanti* in your brother's name to drive away the evil spirit. I even sold my nose ring, the only ornament I had, to pay for it. The astrologer had said that your brother's mind was corrupted due to the bad stars and that he would be all right after the exorcism, but nothing improved your brother."

"Your brother slipped deeper into the habit of drinking, even selling our grains and worn-out utensils. He could not stop drinking. Tsk, tsk! Wherever he went, the trinity — cards, quarrelling, and liquor — would go with him. However, seeing him sometimes on the porch at home, my heart would grow fonder with the thought that at least he had come home, never mind that he would be drunk. I hoped he would improve, but after returning to normal for a while, he would again slip into the same habit," Rukmana's voice cracked.

"Mother, when are we going to the next place? No one can kill us there, can they?" asked the girl, who was not old enough to know her mother's feelings well.

"Sleep, honey! It seems it is already midnight. Sleep. We don't notice the passing of night because of the moonlight," Rukmana patted her daughter lightly.

Awhile later, a bright light fell on Rukmana's face and she woke up.

"Hey! Who is sleeping here? You're inside the cave, and we're here outside? This is unfair. Who is that sleeping with you? Your daughter? Well, there are thirteen of us. Wake your daughter up and come out," a robust youth commanded, peering at Rukmana.

"Please don't kill us. We have nothing. We will leave this place early in the morning and go somewhere else," Rukmana pleaded.

"Mother, what happened? What is that light? Who are you speaking with?" Muna woke up, rubbing her eyes.

"Wait! Let me go first. I am the one who saw them first and told you," said a second youth, who was staggering to his feet beside the first and was now trying to remove the boulder from the cave's mouth.

"Listen, I have already warned you not to tell anyone about us being here. Our friends would jump with joy if they saw these women. They've already drunk enough *raksi*, haven't they?" said the first youth to the second.

"Raski? We've drunk it all right and some are still drinking from the bottle, lying all over the ground," the second youth said, his speech slurred.

"Drag them out quickly," he yelled, his head lolling drunkenly.

Removing the boulder from the mouth of the cave, the first youth grabbed Rukmana's legs and dragged her outside. She pressed her daughter tightly to her chest. She looked timidly at the man's face, like a terrified doe.

Thereafter, the frantic cries of Muna and Rukmana tore the night's silence, seeking help from the entire universe.

"Hey! Those voices sound like my mother's and sister's," a third youth, who was gulping down liquor and leaning against a tree just a stone's throw from the cave, stood on his staggering legs and tottered towards the sound.

"Tsk! These days whenever he hears the voice of any woman he thinks she is his mother or sister. Has he gone mad? Hey! Don't go there now. Let our turn come first." A fourth youth, who had been guzzling alcohol, placed his hands on the third youth's shoulders, trying to stop him.

"No. For God's sake, I'm telling the truth. Let me go and see. It sounds like my mother and sister. If it is, I'll shoot everyone. Let me go!" he shouted vehemently, throwing off the hands of his friend who was still trying to stop him.

Just then a gunshot sounded; a bullet pierced the third youth's temple.

****

Three days after the incident, a man was en route to a foreign country when his eyes fixed on a ghastly sight of three dead bodies—a woman, a teen and a child—somewhere deep in the jungle.

"Ugh! Whose corpses could these be? Which group might have killed them? What were their crimes?"

Many unanswerable questions overpowered him. He looked around and walked on.

*****

KHAGENDRSANGRAULA (1946)

Born in Subhang of Panchthar district in eastern Nepal, Khagendra Sangraula has made his name as a political critic, short-story writer, essayist, novelist, translator, and teacher. This versatile writer has authored five story collections. They are *Nalekhiyeko Itihas* (Unwritten History, 1979), *Handighopteko Jitbajee* (Achievement of a Ravenous Person, 1984), *Seteko Sansar* (Sete's World, 1984), *Hastakshep* (Interfere, 1996), and *Mai Diwas* (May Day, 1997). His novels are *Chetanako Pahilo Dank* (The First Flash of Awareness), *Aamako Chhatpati* (Mother's Restlessness), and *Junkiriko Sangit* (Music of a Glow-worm) while *Janaandolanka Chharraharu* (Waves of the People's Revolution), *Ghoda, Ishwar Ra Mera Ba* (Horse, God and My Father), *Samjhanako Ainaka Tasbirharu* (The Pictures from Memory's Mirror) and *Samjhanaka Kuinetaharu* (The Zigzags of Memory) are his essay collections. Sangraula has been honored with many awards and prizes. The Mainali Story Prize (1989) and Krishnamani Literature Prize (1997) are two of them.

Khagendra Sangraula is a favorite writer of many readers because his writing speaks the truth to many people. He uses simple language to write about reality. He practices his credo "Don't lie when you write." Regarding his writing, Mohanraj Sharma and Rajendra Subedi observe: "Khagendra Sangraula has appeared as a forerunner of contemporary literature suited to Nepali people." His present story *Hareramki Aama* (Hareram's Mother) focuses on an old woman's lamentation for her son after he has been gunned down. The distraught mother's sorrow inspires readers' sympathy.

Hareram's Mother

It was the month of *Chaitra*. The Turture brook was gurgling over slippery rocks. Flowing between the sandy banks, the brook was as negligible as a few strands of hair left on a balding head. A dead body was lying on the bank. Nearly fifteen meters away from the dead body, clad in military uniform, a man was standing upright with a rifle, wearing a similar uniform. The man seemed to be guarding the dead body, which had been the target of the weapon before its death. Ironically, the same weapon was now protecting the dead body.

A narrow road sprawled along the bank almost two hundred meters away from the brook. Every hour, passenger buses would hurtle towards the scene, kicking up dust and causing the atmosphere to vibrate with fear. They would pass by the scene, piercing the terror-filled silence that blanketed the area. Whenever the vehicles drove closer to the corpse and its guard, their speed would suddenly accelerate and the passengers inside would close their windows to hide themselves from the ghastly sight. There was a thin jungle filled with shrubs above the bank. Some people were looking down fearfully at the corpse, making shields of the shrubs and tree trunks. The onlookers would coil up with fright when a gale of wind shook the tree leaves. They would shrink as the movements of their legs rustled the dry leaves.

The dead body was given tight security as if it was that of a VIP. The corpse lay flat — as lifeless, deserted, and dejected as the sandy bank surrounding it. The guard was determined to diligently protect the body. He, however, had no idea to whom he should show or submit this protection. This is how the value of dead bodies rather than living ones, had risen in the land of Buddha.

With a vibration of limitless fear, a worn out bus passed by the scene. On the steep hillside the breeze moved the leaves of the trees above the onlooker's heads, and the rustling of the dry leaves under their feet stirred their hearts.

Meanwhile, from the edge of the jungle, an old woman stormed towards the dead body as if somebody's house were on fire. The air above the jungle hill filled with a ripple of whispers as words passed from one mouth to the other.

"Look! Look! She must be mad."

"Yes! Yes! She's going to be killed."

Inwardly, the whisperers trembled like the leaves. They shrank with fear as the woman ran ahead.

"Dear God! She's surely going to die."

"She seems to be invited to her own death."

Her feet were bare. The edges of her heels were cracked. Her mane of hair cascaded down around her shoulders. Her sari, worn to tatters, did not fully cover her thighs. The back of her filthy body could be seen through the holes that riddled her blouse. The star-like holes were peeping towards the sky.

"Halt!" the onlookers in the jungle above could clearly overhear the guard's warning. But the word had no effect on her, rather she ran more wildly towards the dead body.

"She must be a mad woman," speculated the confused guard. His insensate rifle did not move.

"Dear! Are you my son?" she wept bitterly, caressing the dead body's hair, which was half covered in water. In a fit of anger, her trembling hands caressed its cheeks. Her hands slowly slipped from its face to its neck, to the blood-soaked chest, and then to its stomach. "Dear son! People throughout the village harped on that it was you. They tried to stop me when I said I would come to see you. They said, 'don't go, otherwise you will also be killed,' on! My Hare! What crime did you commit that deserves this death?" She had reached the depths of sorrow. She covered his face with her own. The corpse was reeking in the heat of the sun, but she was unaware of it.

The guard was standing like a statue with his rifle. He was completely taken aback at the sight and did not know what action to take against the woman in such a condition. Her wailing weakened him within.

"Dear son! My Hare!" she beat her breast, raising her head. "One year has passed since I last saw you. Your unfortunate mother has to see you this way today."

For a while she sat on the sandy bank. She covered her face with her hands. Her wailing ceased. Had she fallen unconscious sitting like this? A cold wave of doubt ran through the guard's mind.

The woman stood up. The mouth of the dead person was open. She put a handful of water into his mouth. Then she staggered to the roadside and brought a flower of *siru* grass. She placed it on his head and bowed, bending her head toward the body.

"Son! You used to bow your head to greet me, but by leaving the world before me today, you made me do it," lamented the distraught mother.

Trembling from head to toe, she stood her full height. She again put a handful of water into the corpse's mouth. "My child! My Hare! I could not put even a spoonful of water into your mouth while your soul was struggling to leave your body. Where had you slipped to till today? Where have you disappeared now?" she bemoaned her son's death.

Now the woman turned towards the direction from which she had come and began to walk. She faltered after a few steps. The guard was just ten meters away. Her eyes zeroed in on him. Then she dramatically stepped towards him.

The guard clutched his rifle and instantly became alert. He was confused. "Look now! She was getting close to him, without any fear or hesitation. "She looks like an old beggar," whispered one of the onlookers. "How do you shoot a helpless woman like this?" thought the confused guard, whose forehead was soaked with sweat. His hands, holding the rifle, started trembling peculiarly. He felt his heart beat in his ears.

"Son!" she accosted him, looking straight in his eyes, "Aren't you Kisne?"

'Oh, damn! How did she know my name?' Kisne wondered.

"You are Kisne, aren't you? I'm asking. That Kisne, Govinde's second son."

Kisne, astonished, looked at her unblinkingly. *'She even knows my father's name. How strange!'*

"Do you not know that Govinde Khatri? The one who has a long scar on his forehead, right here!" she said, pointing to the corner of her forehead with her finger, "You . . . aren't you Kisne, his second son?"

Kisne nodded his head.

Turning her head towards her dead son, the woman recalled something and continued, "Our Hareram and you were the same height. You used to go to school together. You were willing to die for each other when you were in agreement but you would become blind with anger when fighting. Remember?"

"Yes," Kisne said with a gesture of his eyes.

"You two had an eye on Dalli. You were head over heels in puppy love. Do you remember? Yes, I'm speaking about Chature Karki's daughter. She was incomparably beautiful. You would have died for her. But both of you were as insignificant as flies in her eyes. Still, you two continued fighting pointlessly for the same girl. Remember?"

Kisne bent his head, silent.

"And your family migrated perhaps to Madhesh . . . or God knows where when you were studying in grade eight or something like that. After your family migrated to Madhesh, our Hareram's studies ended because we could not afford them. Then he went to Kathmandu saying that he wanted to see the capital city and to earn money. Did you know that?"

"No," Kisne shook his head.

"He would come home every six months or so from Kathmandu. Sometimes he would say, 'I'm selling almonds.' Sometimes, 'I'm breaking gravel.' Sometimes 'Lifting loads,' sometimes 'Selling things on the roadside.' He was always jumping and changing from slipshod jobs, without a decent earning. Son! He could not even bring a penny home. He worked hard, but that could not fill his belly alone." She pondered and then backtracked, "Oh, it would be unfair to say that he did not bring anything home. Yes, he brought things. Sometimes he brought a lungi and a shawl, sometimes sandals and a sari. Yes, they were his total earnings . . ."

Her voice cracked. Her eyes fixed on the dead body. "My dear Hare! How kind you were!" she murmured and wiped her tears with her index finger. "Kisne, you joined the military. Didn't you meet him in Kathmandu?"

Kisne shook his head *no*.

"Listen, Kisne! Then he was fed up with Kathmandu. 'That Kathmandu is actually a heaven for the rich and a hell for the poor, Mother. I will no longer go to that hell,' he said. He quit his studies when we could not afford them. I found him changed ever since. With no sign of annoyance, refusal, or unhappiness, my Hare became a completely different person. I feared that he would go mad. But later, he quietly disappeared from home.

I asked everyone, searched everywhere, but could not find a trace of him. At last I learned that he must have headed to the jungle with some people. Sometimes party leaders and sometimes police used to come to the house and threaten me. 'Either show us your son or lose your life.' It was one night last year when my son appeared at home out of nowhere. He was with four people: two males and two females. Oh, for heaven's sake one of them was the same girl—Dalli, Chature Karki's daughter. Yes, the Dalli of yours."

Kisne became nostalgic as he listened to the story about Dalli.

"I was surprised! It was like a dream. I prodded Hare's shoulder and took him aside. 'Rascal! Has Dalli eloped with you?' I asked.

"He just gave a succinct reply, 'No,' trying to dismiss my suspicion. 'She is a friend and her husband hated her. In return, she left him,' he said after a short pause. Hare's mother continued, "Their gestures made me think that they were husband and wife.

But when I observed their activities from a different angle, I could find no trace of it. I was in the kitchen cooking the rice and gundruk soup for them. Poor things, they wolfed down the meal with relish!

"Kisne, I was very impatient to talk with him more. But they did not stop talking until I fell into a deep sleep. Soon I found myself waking up, but only after they had gotten up before me with the rooster's crow in the early morning. I, the idiot, was startled only when Hare said, 'Mother, we're leaving. Don't worry.' I could only talk that much with my son, and that was my luck. He left home promising that he would come for Dashain to receive *tika* from me. Dashain came, but he didn't."

She wiped her tears with the back of her hand.

"Kisne!" she spoke vehemently and pressed his hand that was clutching the rifle hard. "Tell me. Is it you who shot my son?"

Kisne threw her hand off. The left corner of his mouth grimaced strangely. His shoulders shrugged with an expression of sudden fear. His lips fluttered as if they wanted to say something. He could not utter a word. He felt tired, and his weary eyes were fixed on the hot sand.

Then she grabbed Kisne's arm and asked, "Tell me, did you kill your friend?"

"He is a terrorist," Kisne abruptly opened his mouth.

"Don't call him that," she protested innocently, "He is my son. His name is Hare, and in school he was called Hareram Jaisi. Did you forget?"

"He is a terrorist."

"Tell me," she shook his shoulder with force, "Tell me, was it you who killed my son?"

"I'm in the service of the government. Why should I not shoot him when he targets the government?"

"Kisne!" she spoke with growing anger, "He was your close friend. To me you were no different than he was. You used to open your hands asking for something to eat. I would give you whatever I had cooked. The only difference between you two was that he had sucked my breast and you had not. Otherwise there was no difference between you and my Hare. Both of you are my sons. Tell me, Kisne, did you kill him? Tell me quick," she shook his shoulders. "My Hare used to say that he would rebuild the nation, earn his name by uprooting injustice and corruption. Speak up, Kisne, what wrong had he done to you?"

"I'm a soldier bound to the government."

"Kisne!" she shouted, "Didn't your heart ache while shooting him?"

Overcome with confusion and nervousness, Kisne pushed her back. She was knocked forward and fell on the ground, tripping on the body's hands and legs. Looking at her son's dead body, she began to sob.

Kisne felt embittered. He blew his nose. His heart was beating unusually.

"Get up," he shouted. "Get off at once and plead with the leaders of the village or with our commander."

"Why?" the woman turned her head towards him.

"Claim the body and conduct its final rites."

"I don't have even a penny, Kisne. How can I conduct its final rites?"

"Ask for a donation. That will be enough for the final rites and a little will be left over for you as well."

The old woman muttered to herself, *'There were grown up daughters, and they all followed their husbands. My husband was killed while he was guarding the cowshed of the VDC ward chairman. Then, Kisne...'* Her voice broke out from an abyss of pain, "My Hare was also killed. Tell me what alms shall I have to beg for just to get this dead body now??

****

Kisne realized that he was derelict in his duty. *I have forgotten my duty,* he said to himself, becoming alert. *I said what I shouldn't have! Has anyone seen? Or heard?* He became apprehensive. He was terrified. His body was covered with sweat. He grabbed his rifle and shouted, "Halt!" He felt like aiming his weapon at the woman, but his trembling hands could not follow his own orders.

Words like halt did not scare Hare's mother. Instead, she continued muttering, "My son had never wronged anyone. How boldly and beautifully he would say, 'I will rebuild the nation by clearing up the injustice and tyranny and earn my name.' Did you not hear him saying this, Kisne?"

"Get lost, nonsense woman."

Hare's mother got up and moved in the direction from which she had come. She was tired, weak, and burning with grief. It seemed that even a small gust of wind could easily blow her to the ground. Trembling and tottering, she moved ahead and let out a deep sigh. After reaching the bank of the brook, she tumbled over with her face down. She did not make a move, but after sometime she slowly raised her head. Her eyes were in a daze and then they fixed on her dead son.

"Hare! What mistake did you make that warranted your death? How boldly you used to say, 'I will rebuild the nation, end injustice and tyranny, and earn my name.' To the person, who talked so nicely, they. . ."

"Stop!"

The warning had no effect on her. She did not stop. She was muttering. "Kisne! What wrong did my Hare do to you? Why do you not respond, rascal? Did you shoot him to settle your old feud because he had finally won Dalli? Why do you not speak up, are you mute?"

Now the real Kisne completely vanished within himself and the dutiful guard came out. He felt that government witnesses were spying on him from everywhere. "Oh God! I am ruined," he grieved, "I failed to secure my government job. What will happen to me now?" Nervous, he pointed his rifle at her chest and fired. A big hole in her body! She was hurled towards the brook, and she fell down, stretching her hands and legs. The gunshot sent a ripple of fear through the crowd of onlookers who were hiding behind the bushes and tree trunks in the jungle above. They cowered with fear.

A stream of blood from the woman's chest flowed up to the water of the gurgling brook. A lock of Hare's hair was submerged in the water.

Breaking the dreadful silence, which was suffocating under the terrible shadow of death, the brook Turture flowed continuously with its rhythmic ripples. The wind blew sonorously.

*****

PADMAVATISINGH (1948)

Padmavati Singh was born in the capital city of Kathmandu. She has worked for organizations dedicated to women's health, education, and empowerment, which she says are the sources of her short stories. Her collections of stories include *Samayadamsha* (This Sting of Time, 2011), *Mauna Swikriti* (Silent Submission, 2008), *Padmavati Singhka Kathaharu* (Stories of Padmavati Singh, 2000), *Kathakar* (The Storyteller, 1987), Kathayam (Storyscape, 1982) and *Kathadi* (Story Line, 1981). Her book *Samanantar Aakash* (Parallel Sky, 2005) was translated into English. This Sajha Prize-winning novel calls for "an equal share of the sky" for women. Padmavati has been honored with many prizes including the Devkota Century Gold Medal (2010).

"The realities behind women's lives are revealed in Padmavati's stories. Women struggle to establish their identity and to protect their womanhood," observes Dr. Dayaram Shrestha. The president of the women's literary association *Gunjan*, Padmavati says that her focus while writing stories is to "draw a lively picture of the country and time, as much as the ultimate truth of life and the world." The following story, *Himsako Maunata* (The Silence of Violence), centers on a displaced woman who suffers the double tragedy of losing her husband during a Maoist-Government battle, and is later raped. The author presents a harrowing picture of women in war-torn Nepal, focusing on women's rights and equality.

The Silence of Violence

The night was still. Darkness had enveloped the village. The brook thundered down the gorge, adding horror to the night. Nirmaya, distraught and restless, tossed and turned in her bed. It was not only this night; she had passed many such agitated nights. Fear and premonitions of evil churned in her mind. The cause of her anguish was her husband, Bam Bahadur, who had been missing ever since the crossfire with rebels. Whether he had been kidnapped or killed, or had been hiding somewhere after escaping from their capture, she did not know. The authorities had neither confirmed him dead nor alive. She felt burned alive, like a fish sizzling over coals in the fireplace.

Neighbors sympathized with her, but their words only added fuel to the fire. They did not give her any relief. The edges of her heart crumbled, and tears of anguish flowed from the corners of her eyes. Trying to console her, Master Baje in the next house had said, "Many people who disappeared during the crossfire have returned safe and sound; therefore, don't lose your hope, Nirmaya ..."

He had also said, "If Bam Bahadur has been kidnapped, he will return after his release sure enough." So Nirmaya, too, had not given up. She lit the lamp of hope, stretching her eyes towards the path along which he might come.

****

Tearing the silence of the still night, the painful howling of the old woman next door shook the hearts of the neighbors. Who knows if a similar tragedy might befall someone else tomorrow? Bire, the woman's only son, had been killed by security personnel a few days ago. She had not known her son was a rebel. He had gone to town under the influence of his friends, in the hope of getting a job. Hearing the tragic news from her son's friends, the woman began to fall apart, wailing continuously. Her sorrowful howling, "*Kanchho . . . Kanchho . . .*" was heard all around. It seemed that the cloudy sky melted into rain and started pouring. The entire woods and hills seemed to be shedding tears to accompany her grief but nothing could pull her from her ocean of misery. All the villagers would approach her but returned leaving their words of sympathy. Those words were only formalities to her, while she was scorched like grains kept under the glaring sun. Who would uproot the nail that was embedded deep in her heart and smeared with blood?

"Whose evil eyes fell on this beautiful village, this peaceful country?" Nirmaya asked herself with a heavy heart. The village looked deserted even in the day. All the villagers huddled in their homes out of fear. The village's school, health post, police post, and a few government offices had been demolished in the crossfire between the security personnel and the rebels just a few days ago. An inexpressible fear of another possible attack and confrontation was reflected in the villager's eyes. For them, each night had been a *kalratri* — a night of complete annihilation. For Nirmaya, the night's fearful silence had been a sleeping volcano before an eruption.

"Hey! Open the door!" a harsh male voice tore the night's silence, shaking her grief-stricken heart.

"Who on earth has come this late at night? Oh God! What misfortune might befall me now?" Muttering a curse and trembling with fear, Nirmaya got up abruptly from her bed.

"Will you open the door or shall I break it down?" another loud voice roared. After a while, two rebels barged into her house. "Where? Where the hell have the people of this house gone?" yelled one.

Frightened, Nirmaya retreated to her bed. "Hey, get up. We're hungry. Cook whatever you have. Feed us," ordered the other man.

Nirmaya silently got up and began to make a fire in the oven. Soon the meal was ready. The men ate until they were full and then laid on a mattress near the oven. One said, "We'll stay here today." The other yawned and said, "Today we have shelter and enough food. Where will we go tomorrow?"

"There is no point in worrying about tomorrow for those who wander with an uncertain future at hand," the next said, lighting a *bindi.*

"Where's the water jug?" one roared, looking Nirmaya over from head to toe. She washed all the plates and then filled a jug of water, pouring it from a pitcher, and placed it before them. When she was about to turn around to go to her bed, one of them caught her hand and asked, "Where is your police husband? He often comes to sleep with you, doesn't he?" The room was filled with a lewd laughter. Nirmaya looked at them hatefully and said, "You might have killed him. He has been missing since the last clash."

"Tch . . . tch . . . tch . . . Gone missing? What happens if he has gone missing? Then, you can take us as your husband!" one of them said and pushed the corner of her sari into her mouth before forcing her to the floor, while the next stripped her naked and fulfilled his barbarous desire. Then, having coarsely used her body, the two criminals left the scene. The villagers, who were sleeping wrapped in the loneliness of the night, did not hear the sound of the ruthless attack on Nirmaya. No one heard the shrieking cry of her soul. Even her elderly father-in-law and the others sleeping upstairs did not respond to her agony. They lay in their beds, cowering nervously.

Lying like a log on the floor, the terrified and anguished

Nirmaya endured a mountain of pain. An endless sea of grief started to pour from her eyes. Her tolerance had reached its limits and was crumbling into pieces. She saw herself naked. In the silence of the violence, she felt the rape like an ocean of pain surging inside her belly, and she pressed it hard with both her hands before she fell to the floor and fainted. The blood flowed from between her legs. The three-month-old fetus that was in her womb died an unnatural death. Regaining her consciousness, Nirmaya found herself weltered in a pool of blood. Making every effort, she screamed in agony but no one came to see her plight, not even her father-in-law. She tried to stand but collapsed on the floor, unconscious.

Nirmaya found herself in a hospital bed when her eyes opened. She had been unconscious when Master Baje, ever helpful and kind to all, came to her after he heard her crying. She survived by the grace of Master Baje, who rushed her to the hospital.

Nirmaya broke down when she saw Master Baje and a few villagers in the hospital. She started to wail as if each ounce of pain was being squeezed from her heart. All of them understood why she was crying, but spoke nothing, realizing that there was no point in crying over something that had already come to pass. They just bent their heads and looked at each other. When they were about to go, leaving her at the hospital, Nirmaya joined both her hands and pleaded, "Baje, if I die, everything is over. If I live, I'll never go back to the village. Please, let me know if my husband comes home."

****

A few days later, Nirmaya was sent to a rehabilitation center for conflict victims. Master Baje was informed of this in the village after Nirmaya requested word be sent. In the center, she saw women and children of different ages taking shelter like she was

— all suffering from either physical disabilities or psychological trauma. She felt that it was not blood, but a river of agony that flowed through her veins when she found herself among these people rendered homeless by the conflict. All seemed to be wracked by the silence of violence, helpless, as if they were being led down the road of an uncertain future. Hopelessness, grief, and anguish spilled from everyone's eyes. Nirmaya was filled with consolation and sympathy at the plight of the women and children at the center. '*Who is responsible for the nightmarish condition of these people?*' she asked herself. No one had the answer.

Nirmaya listened to the tale of Bishnumaya, who was also in the center.

Bishnumaya had had a happy life with her husband and two children. One night rebels barged into her house and, suspected her husband of spying, and slit his throat in front of her. A gang of rebels had been guarding her house. It did not matter that her husband was innocent; he was killed when one of his enemies reported him.

Likewise, the rebels set Ramaniya's house ablaze and drove her family out of her village. Prior to this, her husband had been warned to quit his job, but he denied the order. Later her husband's whereabouts and condition were unknown. She had been living a wretched life like an outlaw with her two children.

Lakhkhidevi, another conflict victim, had been mentally distraught since the abduction of her two sons. From then on, she had been living a hopeless life with her little daughter.

A more heartrending story was that of Malakhamai. Aged around twenty-five, she spoke to no one. She only looked around doubtfully and hollered all the time. She developed a fitful habit—sometimes bursting into laughter or weeping, while at other times running around wildly. Her son, Malakha, narrated the tale of how his mother came to this condition.

"The police were chasing my father. Mother was cooking rice. Father went to hide himself under a haystack after the police shot at him. Then the police set the piles of hay on fire. Father died, burned alive. That scene deeply shocked my mother and she went mad."

Nirmaya kept the woman's six-year-year old, Malakha, with her at all times because he was afraid to be near his own mother.

The story of Pawankali was no less heartrending. It was broad daylight when a gang came and dragged her into a cornfield. They raped her and left there, stark naked. After this she could not bear the hateful eyes of the villagers and ran to the city. Even in the city she was sexually harassed. Finally, she came to take shelter in the center.

All the women in the rehabilitation center had their own heartrending tales. Nirmaya felt that her pain assuaged listening to the harrowing tales of others. Some women had been victimized by the rebels, while the others were the victims of police atrocities. Those most affected in the grinding clashes were women and children. The state and the rebels were both blindly exercising their power through their criminal activities—murder, violence, abduction and rape. There were also the women who had faced gruesome torture from both sides. The country was sinking deeper into mire. Nirmaya's heart shattered to see the plight of the country. Her heart ached at its pain. The whole country was taking a blood bath of murder, violence, and rape.

Nirmaya pined for her hillocks and hillsides. Her village surrounded by hills, woods, streams, and rivulets danced in her eyes. In her vision, rhododendrons blossomed all over the hill. The *peeplechautari* and *deurali* came alive in her mind. *'I wonder whether I shall go there some day'* her heart burst with the feeling of suffocation.

"This conflict ruined the lives of many people. Who has benefited from this conflict? Who will compensate us for the human casualties, and rebuild the damaged infrastructure? When will the murder, violence, and destruction end?"

****

While Nirmaya was mulling over these thoughts and staring at the setting sun behind a distant hill, Master Baje appeared before her out of nowhere.

"Nirmaya! Are you all right?"

Nirmaya's face lit up a bit, seeing him unexpectedly.

"Look there, Nirmaya," he said, pointing towards the door.

Nirmaya was overjoyed upon seeing her husband. She ran towards him as if her feet were floating above the floor.

"I knew you would return," she said with tearful eyes.

"But . . . who are you?" came the question—the twist of the knife in Nirmaya's suffering.

"I'm Nirmaya . . . Your wife . . . Yes . . . Your wife . . . !" she stammered.

Confused, her husband looked at Master Baje and asked, "Uncle! Who is she? I don't know her!"

Nirmaya's eyes filled with the tears of misery.

"Don't worry," said Master Baje sympathetically. "Now, your husband doesn't know anyone. He suffered a deep head injury

45

in the clash, and all the memories of his past have been buried under darkness. The memories of his past have disappeared in the mist of forgetfulness. Someone found him seriously injured. He was then rescued and admitted to the hospital. Thank God, he is saved, but he is a different person now."

"And how did he know you?"

"He doesn't know me either. He addresses me as 'Uncle' because the man who brought him to the village introduced me as his uncle."

Nirmaya, with her heavy heart, looked at her husband. Her eyes were full of tears. The same bright face, same sturdy body—no other changes, except his unacquainted look, which had no sense of familiarity.

Indifferent to his wife's steady gaze of love, Bam Bahadur left the place quietly.

Nirmaya stood aghast. She kept staring at her husband, who shone like a moon that soon disappeared from a horizon. She could not cry or speak, nor could follow him. Only the sound of silence echoed all around her. She looked on silently with her vacuous eyes, as if she were in a silent protest from deep inside that would burn and explode one day to become a volcano in support of the citizens. The citizens who had forgotten to laugh, whose smile had been seized, who had been killed, or who had fallen prey to violence.

*****

BHAGIRATHISHRESTHA (1948)

One of the forerunners of Nepali short-story writing, Bhagirathi Shrestha was born in Gulmi district, western Nepal. To date, she has published six collections of short stories. They are *Kramasha* (Gradually, 1986), *Mohadamsha* (The Sting of Love, 1987), *Bibhram* (Illusion, 1989), *Rangin Pokhari* (The Colorful Pond, 1993), *Bhumigat* (Underground, 2005), and *Rato Gulaf* (The Red Rose, 2009). Her first book was *Malati,* a novel, published in 1978. *Yasto Euta Aakas* (One Such Sky, 1990) was her second novel. She was awarded the Ratna Shree Gold Medal, the Mainali Story Prize, the Devkota Century Gold Medal, and others.

Bhagirathi's stories portray female experiences, the country's adverse politico-economic condition, and the inescapable situations that befall individuals, families, and society. She says, "The sensitive issues or events such as social, political, economic and familial situations that relate to women inspire me to write." Of Bhagirathi's story writing, Ghataraj Bhattarai comments: "[T]he strongest side of Bhagirathi is her ability to mingle the mental state of male or female characters with the values of society to weave them into engrossing stories by highlighting the male or female character's various problems and related issues." Her story, *Safaya* (Execution), was set during the time when the country submerged in political unrest, portrays a family's helplessness over the dilemma faced by the main character.

Execution

Bhashkar Sharma wakes up suddenly from his fitful sleep during the night's suffocating heat when his telephone rings. He has just fallen asleep in the coolness of the morning. He is apprehensive since these are troubling times, and anarchy is looming large around him. So early! Who could it be? Is it good news or bad? He picks up the receiver hesitantly after the phone keeps on ringing. He is relieved when he realizes that it is his friend Amar on the other end and his heartbeat slows.

Amar's frantic voice, full of fear, reaches his ear.

"Bhashkar, I've heard bad news from a reliable source. The rebels are going to root out the district level leaders. I'm told that our names are also on their hit list. Listen! If you're alive, you have everything, if not, you have nothing. So the first thing we need to do is be safe at all possible cost. Tonight I'm going with my wife to live in the city. You must also make arrangements for your safety. Our other friends already prepared to leave the village after I informed them about the list. Don't wait, Bhaskar. They're going to attack us soon."

Bhashkar feels as if the news itself is a mob of terrorists coming to attack him with arms and ammunitions. He keeps silent in his bed. His sick father's voice coming from the next room stabilizes his body and mind. How can he leave his family and housework behind and go to the city for his safety alone? The thought of leaving home breaks his heart.

Meanwhile, Bhashkar's houseman, Shyame, enters the room with tea. Bhashkar rises and sits up in his bed. He begins to sip the tea. "This Shyame would have probably raised a gun and gone to the war front with the rebel soldiers if he had been in his village," he thinks. "Luckily, he is with us in this house instead of with the rebels in the war," Bhashkar concludes, recalling the rebel's policy.

He is the type of person who wishes people well and understands their suffering. In collaboration with his co-workers, he has launched many developmental projects. The paved road, water taps, hospital, electricity, and college: all are the efforts of him and his friends. "If we are in the rebel's bad book despite our constructive works, the objective of the People's War cannot be just and good — nor will it end well. This is nothing but a demonic form of terrorism," he concludes.

Bhashkar sips the tea while looking out the window. 'The LTTE in Sri Lanka led the guerrilla war demanding a separate state and caused the death of thousands of innocent people and high-class social and political dignitaries. The war only brought great destruction on both sides. What is the meaning of that blood? The ongoing People's War in this holy land will also be a fiasco one day. Thousands of women's sindoor has been wiped out, the old-age support for many fathers and mothers is in jeopardy. Their tears will curse the People's War. The rebels attempt to change people's minds by imparting threats and fueling criminal activities. Their activities will bear the seed of hatred, revenge, indignity, malice, and anger among the people, making the situation even worse. Its peace, camaraderie, cooperation, and cordiality that can bring a positive change to the country's development. For how long will the country and its people bear this destructive rage, this damned wild behavior and polluted atmosphere?' Bhashkar wonders.

The sweltering heat of the Terai is so suffocating that it feels as if a boulder is pressing down on him hard from above. Outside his house a crow perches on the branch of a big guava tree and a sound spontaneously comes from Bhashkar's mouth: '*Subol, subol*' willing the bird to caw a good message. He thinks that the bird is signaling an imminent tragedy. It is not as easy for him to leave the house as Amar advised him to do. His father, bedridden by paralysis on the right part of his body; his mother with her heart ailment; his wife and the farms; and the rice mill, he would be leaving them all destitute. How can he leave the house for an uncertain length of time? Though he takes Amar's words seriously, he can't make an immediate decision to leave for the city. His mind is haunted by an unknown fear. *'If I were a bird, I could have saved myself from the threshold of disaster by flying into a nest hanging on a tree,'* he thinks, *'Or if I had supernatural powers, I could have transformed myself into a different person to slip past the rebels.'* But Bhashkar has no option other than to run away to the city. Anything might happen to him at any moment.

He remembers his paternal uncle, Ramnath, a popular district-level leader. The rebels killed him one night after they had locked his family in a room. They tied him to a pillar and mercilessly hacked him with a blade. They had tortured him until he died. Until his last hour of life, Ramnath had pleaded, "Don't kill me. I'd rather hand over all my property to you. I've done nothing wrong." The rebels, however, had only one reply, "We don't need your property. Our policy is to finish off the popular political leaders like you."

After the grisly murder of Ramnath, two rebels shot Bhashkar's maternal uncle, Sagar Sharma, while he was jogging, on the charge that he did not cough up enough donations for their party. Bhashkar remembers the known and unknown people killed on the charges of spying on the People's War, of going against the rebel's policy, declining to give donations, and refusing to send their children to fight. He even remembers those who were killed out of personal malice. How could he remain detached from the cruel current of dirty politics? Recalling the shocking incidents, which are imminent to him and others as well, his mind and body become weak as if death is suffocating him.

"Bhashkar! My boy! Why don't you get out of your bed? I want to go to the toilet."

The voice interrupts Bhashkar's train of thought. His father must be helped to the toilet. With his houseman Shyame's help, he completes his father's morning chores: taking him to the toilet, washing his hands and mouth, changing his clothes, and feeding him milk and medicine. His father's health was worsening. Bhashkar wonders how Shyame will be able to look after his father when Bhashkar is away. What trouble this is! What a difficult situation! A dilemma!

Bhashkar looks out the window. His face is expressionless. The cawing of the crows from the branches of the densely grown silk oak tree once gave him satisfaction, but today he hears only the message of his imminent death. He even feels that the enticing banana, guava, mango, grapefruit, and litchi trees are demons— the movement of even a single leaf shakes his heart. He has no place to hide.

"Why on earth are you staring this way? You haven't taken a bath either. The meal is ready."

Ranju's voice startles Bhashkar. Even a soft sound is loud enough to make him flinch.

He gets out of his bed, as quiet as a mouse, and takes a bath. He enters the kitchen to have his meal. He finds it hard to swallow even a morsel.

Seeing her husband's sad face, Ranju asks, "What? What happened to you? Are you not well? Why are you looking sad? It seems you have no appetite."

"Ranju! A thunderbolt has hit us. It's unsafe for me to live at home. Amar and our friends have already left home for their safety. We spoke on the phone this morning, and Amar said that we district level leaders are going to be killed soon. Tell me Ranju, how can I leave home?" Bhashkar unleashes his embittered feelings.

"What crime have you done to deserve death?" Ranju wonders.

"Being a popular political leader of the district is my crime, Ranju," Bhashkar says regretfully.

"My God, what am I hearing? Under what tyranny are we being ground? This country is cursed. What an evil time has come! Good people either have to be afraid and run away, or face attacks. Well, leave home today. I will face whatever comes. Save your life first. Don't worry about our home. If they're really taking action, they might come at any moment," says Ranju nervously.

"I can't just go to the city empty handed as you have said. If I go, I have to collect money for our son and daughter living in the hotel and for myself. I can stay with relatives for only a few days. I will arrange everything today and leave for the city early in the morning."

Ranju holds her breath when she hears her husband's decision to go to the city.

The dinner is over. The family is watching television. A handbag and a suitcase have already been packed and put in a corner. Bhashkar has collected money for himself. He has promised his father and mother that he will return in a few days.

Today as well Kantipur Television is showing scenes of gory massacres; ordinary people, children, youths, seniors, and security personnel were mercilessly killed by gunmen. The couple's eyes used to well with tears at seeing only one or two corpses on television. Their hearts used to ache. But now they have become hardened, with few feelings and emotions for such tragic events. Their eyes and ears are accustomed to such news these days. They are interested only in the enormity of the damage caused by the rebels: where did they attack, where did they demolish infrastructure, how many security personnel did they kill, how many innocent citizens became martyrs, how many rebels were killed, how many people were abducted, how many were killed for spying, how many were wounded or disabled, and how many have disappeared?

The couple hears a loud bang from the main door downstairs while they are watching the news. Bhashkar thinks that Khime, the houseman living in the small hut adjoining his house, might have opened the door. His ears and eyes grow wary at the sound of footsteps and a humming sound coming from the courtyard. Who is coming at this odd time of night? Are they rebels? Bhashkar trembles with fear and can't think straight. The sound of the footsteps on the wooden ladder becomes clearer. He collapses on the sofa. He is petrified, unable to think. He can't decide where to hide. He is trapped in a net of complexity. His mother and Ranju, who are watching television from the next sofa, begin to shake with fear. Shyame, who is on the floor, also begins to shake.

Two round-faced, narrow-eyed gunmen, and two stout girls clad in combat dress, storm into the room. The family members are ashen with fear and they feel as if their breath has stopped. They see only darkness around them.

"Who on earth has come at this time, son?" comes the voice of Bhashkar's sick father from the next room.

"Shut up, stupid old man. Be quiet," a girl yells out.

Despite having been sick for a long time, Bhashkar's father is aware of the rebel's activities and the country's political situation.

"Please don't harm my only son. I beg you. Do whatever you like to me instead. I don't want to live with this body, blighted with disease," the old man sobs.

"Quiet, old man. If a single word comes out of your mouth,

we'll blow you away," one of the youths explodes.

The room is filled with fear. Bhashkar's mother and wife begin to sob. The frightened Shyame covers his face with his palms while Bhashkar cowers on the sofa.

Bhashkar sees the end of his life in front of these messengers of Death. He will undergo the same treatment as his uncles. His heartbeat quickens and becomes louder as if it is Death knocking at his door.

"You are Bhashkar Sharma, right?" the youth fires the words like bullets.

Bhashkar's faltering spirit revives.

"Yes, but why in God's name are you here? What can I offer you? What do you want?" Bhashkar asks frantically.

"We came to ask you something. Come down first. We will ask there," one of the girls erupts, hurling the words from her mouth as though they were stones.

Bhashkar thinks that his doomsday has arrived and that his head has already fallen into a lion's mouth. *These people are the messengers of Death sent by Yamaraj*, he murmurs.

A burly youth advances towards him. He grabs Bhashkar's right arm firmly and begins to drag him out of the room. Bhashkar has no strength; he is unable to rise or walk. He feels like a log being dragged.

His shell-shocked mother starts to sob and firmly catches hold of her son's arm and tries to pull him towards her. "Where are you taking my son? Take me. Kill me, but do nothing to him."

"Eh, why are you shouting? Get inside the room," one of the girls yells, hitting her with the muzzle of her gun. Then the girl pushes the old woman into the room and closes the door from outside.

"Please don't do anything to my husband. If anything happens to him, our family will be ruined. I would rather give you whatever you ask," Ranju pleads, grabbing onto the girl's legs.

The other girl drags Ranju towards her and pushes her into the room as well. "If you shout or weep loudly, you'll pay for it. Don't you know our power? We haven't come to show you kindness, love, or mercy," the girl shouts, shutting the door.

The rebels fall on Bhashkar, pushing and kicking, and take him out of his house. The entire atmosphere emits a scent of death. He feels as though the envoys of Yamaraj are tying him up and taking him to a slaughterhouse. He expects his *haruwacharuwas* to run towards him with sickles, spears, axes, and *khurpa* to fight them off. Bhashkar's voice chokes up as he tries to shout for help.

They take him to the courtyard. Complete silence is all around. His sweater is soaked with sweat. The air is still. No sound comes from the trees; not even a single leaf moves. It seems that they are all mourning the imminent death of their owner. The children of Bhashkar's domestic helpers can be heard whimpering and huddling together in their nearby huts. The wealth that Bhashkar earned from his toil over many years, the trees he reared, and his domestic workers, friends, relatives, and fellow villagers are all useless in this moment of urgency. Bhashkar sees guns and *khukuris* glittering from the rebel's waists in the moonlit night.

His mind reels. "I'm the only son of my parents. You saw their disabled condition. In my life I have always done good things for people. Please don't do anything—for the sake of my family. I have to live for them. I would rather give you whatever you ask," Bhashkar begs in a last-ditch attempt for life.

His own nervousness weakens him.

"Yes, we know you've done nothing wrong. But you're an influential leader of this district. We're punishing you because we're taking out such leaders, and your name is on our list. It is our party's policy. Your pleading has nothing to do with us. We're committed to the orders of our high command, and we must carry out our party's policy," a robust youth gives a briefing of the reasons for Bhashkar's death.

"Then kill me in a single shot. Don't use the *khukuri*," Bhashkar pleads.

The next youth jumps over him.

"Beggars can't be choosers. We won't kill you as you wish. We are not here to show you mercy. We only know our high command's order."

Bhashkar's pleading is engulfed by the fearsome mouth of Death that now stands before him.

All around the messengers of Yamaraj.

The foreboding silence of death.

The helpless shadow of time.

The boiling point of terror.

The guns and knives hang from the messenger's waists, glimmering in the moonlight. A *khukuri* lands on Bhashkar from a girl's hand. He tries to block the thrust with his right hand. Three fingers fall on the ground.

"Oh God!" he cries in pain and, almost losing consciousness, falls to the ground. Blood wells up from his wound and flows around him.

Another youth pulls the trigger of his gun, which emits two gunshot sounds, leaving two holes, one in Bhashkar's temple and the other in his chest. Then a complete silence . . .

An influential person, who had been on the rebel's hit list, is thus executed in his beloved courtyard.

A continuous wailing is heard from the room upstairs. After the cruelest slaughter, the envoys of Yamaraj start towards the dark forest in a victorious mood.

*****

GHANASHYAMDHAKAL (1954)

Born in Syangja district, in western Nepal, Ghanashyam Dhakal is a versatile writer who has authored several novels and books of essays, poems, short stories, and literary criticism. To date, he has published five collections of short stories. They are *Bhariya Ra Yatri* (Porter and Traveller, 1990), *Sahid Manachitrama Napareko Sahid* (The Martyr Missing from the Martyr List, 1992), *Samarpanko Batoma* (On the Way to Sacrifice, 1995), *Aajako Mahabharat* (Mahabharat Today, 1999) and *Shahidko Salik* (A Martyr's Statue, 2010). *Nam Kamaune Raharma* (Hankering after Fame, 1986) and *Daridrata Bata Mukti* (Liberation from Poverty, 1989) are his essay collections. *Gaonbhitra* (Inside the Village, 1991) and *Rato Aakash* (The Red Sky, 2004) are his novels and *Ganga-Kaberi Express* (1986) and *Abhibadan Garchha Sagarmatha Perubhiyali Janakrantilai* (Mount Everest Salutes the Peruvian Revolution, 1988) are his collections of long narrative poems.

A Marxist writer, Dhakal raises a voice against exploitation, suppression, and discrimination through his stories. Dr. Devi Prasad Gautam writes: "There is a real picture of poverty in Dhakal's stories. He has sympathetically presented the life of people who are destined to be exploited and victimized out of illiteracy and inescapable situations." Chairman of both the All Nepal Writers' Association and the Progressive Writers' Association, Dhakal was honored with the literary prizes *Rastriya Pratibha Puraskar, Parijat Srijan Puraskar, Sahitya Sandhya Puraskar,* and others. He prefers writing socialist realist stories, for they "expose the underlying truth" and help to transform society. Taken from his collection, *Shahidko Salik,* the story *Pachhuto* (Remorse) presents the plight of a poor farmer who is abducted and consequently killed by security personnel against the backdrop of the Maoist-Government war in Nepal.

Remorse

Gopal came out of his house in the morning when the rain, which had been pelting down throughout the night, stopped. Except for a drizzle, there had not been heavy rain for the past fifteen days or so. Water was splashing everywhere after it welled up on the steep foothills. The waterfalls, whitened by the strength of the water, cascaded down the hills, both straight and serpentine. It looked as though Mother Earth was squeezing her breast and releasing streams of milk.

It was unlikely that the sun would shine as a shawl of cloud blotted it out, narrowing the great depth of the sky. The forest and trees were green. The weather below the hills was picture perfect, while the hilltops above were completely covered with mist. It was the end of Asadh, the month of the monsoon.

"If only the paddy could be planted . . . If it cannot be done this time also . . . ," Gopal said doubtfully with the faintest hint of hope. By this time during the past two years, the paddy saplings would have been planted already and would have grown green. But only the velvety dubo grass grew in the paddy field this time. The young paddy saplings had been left lying in the seedling beds and were growing old. The plan of planting the paddy was simply hoping against hope. There was no certainty that it could be done.

An event from twenty days earlier danced before Gopal's eyes as if it happened yesterday.

****

At that time also, an abundant amount of water was splashing everywhere. Since Gopal's land was in a steep area, the paddy had to be planted by guiding small channels of trickling water towards the field. Yoking their oxen, the farmers were scattered across the field. In the rush of work, they were so busy that they hardly had time to talk to each other. Gopal, too, was busy working. No sooner had he yoked the oxen than he heard the whir of a helicopter above him in the sky. He saw the helicopter skimming over them, making three or four rounds. The farmers felt as if their ears were deafened by the sound. The scared oxen bellowed and tried to run from their yokes. A few oxen broke free and ran wildly with their tails raised high. The helicopter landed in the meadow nearby. As the helicopter's whirring stopped, its door opened and rifle-holding policemen jumped down, one after the other.

"I don't think they're here for a good reason," Gopal thought. Seeing the police around them, the frightened farmers guessed that something bad was happening. Nowadays police are 'equal to death or disappearance', they used to say.

"Are these the ones we're looking for?" asked one of the rifle-holders.

"Yes, these are the terrorists trying community farming," said the next.

Then the police made a dash towards the farmers, firing their rifles indiscriminately. Only a few farmers had time to release their oxen from their yokes. Gopal ran towards the jungle. It was a close shave when a bullet whizzed past his ear. He stumbled to the ground but quickly got up and ran faster. He slowed his steps and looked back when he was certain that the police were not behind him. He saw two of his neighbors being dragged away.

In the evening, Gopal returned to his home, but his arrested neighbors did not. They did not return the next day or the day after. There was a ripple of gossip about the missing pair, but the villagers were kept in the dark about their whereabouts. Seven days later, the villagers were told that two dead bodies were found floating in the Marsyangdi. They assumed that the bodies were those of the missing. But how did they get there? Who threw them? What condition were they in? Whose bodies could they be? Nobody knew. No one was allowed to look at them. Thereafter, riot police stepped up their mobilization in the village and scoured the area daily. In such a situation, no one dared to yoke his oxen again.

"Why should we be dying for cultivating the field while others have left barren?" said Gopal's wife, Buddhikala. And yet she was afraid of a possible recurrence of earlier events. Obviously, their land would not give a sufficient yield. However, from that yield she could have managed to feed her children *jaulo* for about six months of the year. She could even feed her guests.

"Even so, why leave the field uncultivated? For how long shall we manage on grain from the shops? I wonder if Kusale Kanchho is at home now. If one more person were here the oxen could be yoked," Gopal said. Buddhikala reluctantly agreed with her husband. It took the whole morning for the couple to find helping hands to cultivate the field.

They began to plant the paddy amidst the silence around them. Their calls to muster the oxen—"*Ho! Ho!*"—were heard far and wide. There was not even a shepherd around. The sky was not clear yet. Under the stillness of the moonlit night, five pairs of hands could be seen working intently in the field. Every now and then, Gopal turned his head to look around. He became confident upon seeing no one. "They didn't come yesterday. If they come only one day, make it today . . ." He again turned his head and stretched his eyes far away into the distance.

"Damn those sons of bitches! How could they not be coming?" he thundered angrily, cursing his helpers. The farmers were shocked.

"Hey! Hey! Untie the oxen—why did you yoke them?" the policemen came towards them, shouting.

"Why should we release them?" Gopal protested.

"Gathering and community farming aren't allowed here."

"We're cultivating our own field. We're not holding any meeting or gathering."

"Look! What a good speech he gives. He seems to be a leader of terrorists. Boys, bring him in line if he disobeys," the sub-inspector shouted in anger.

"OK. OK. Wait. We will release the oxen," Buddhikala hurriedly freed the oxen. The sub-inspector racked his brain and twitched his head as if he remembered something. A feeling that he had seen Gopal somewhere surged within him. Gopal, who had put on gray half pants and a country-made checkered t-shirt, was in his early thirties. Tall and long-faced with a slightly pointed nose, Gopal was dark skinned. It would not be difficult to recognize him because of his thick eyebrows. Obviously, the sub-inspector had seen him at a protest rally of farmers.

Gopal returned home, maddened with anger. "Thank God they did not kill us," Buddhikala exclaimed, and she felt relieved for they were safe. She looked like one who returns home after winning a battle. Despite that, her heart was filled with fear.

Nobody could say with certainty when or to whom tragedy might strike. Gopal yawned and looked towards the western sky, counting the remaining days of the monsoon. A patch of blue sky was visible through a rift in the cloud and the sunrays filtered through. When it was completely dark, a stranger appeared at Gopal's yard asking, "Can I buy a little ghee?" He didn't look like an ordinary person.

"No, we don't have any. Who sent you here saying we have ghee?" Buddhikala spoke coldly.

"This is not a man who came with good intentions," she concluded after he had left.

"I don't think they will let us live at home now," Gopal remarked.

Buddhikala's head spun. An unknown fear made her blood run cold. She suddenly became absorbed in thought and agreed with her husband, "It's better to leave here very soon than fall prey to them."

"What's the use of hurrying away without consulting our friends?" Gopal said.

"Father, when shall we plant our paddy?" his daughter interrupted.

"We'll plant some other day, when the police don't come," Gopal tried to pacify his daughter's curiosity. Then she fell asleep on her father's lap. Gopal put her to bed, and the couple talked before they went to sleep late at night.

The world did not belong to them only; others too were active in the darkness outside. It must have been midnight when Buddhikala woke up to the sound of footsteps in the yard. After a moment, the lights of torches glimmered outside.

"Wake up, my love! The police have come." She shook her husband. The arrival of the police, whether during the day or the night, was not uncommon. It had been a common occurrence for the villagers to see the police raiding their houses under the pretext of searching for someone hiding.

Knocking came from the door.

"Who is that at this ungodly hour?" Gopal demanded.

"Please open the door. We are from the police station."

Gopal got out of his bed and opened the door. The policemen entered with torches. Buddhikala lit the *tuki* lamp. This time the policemen did not search for anything in the corners of the house as they had on their previous raids. They did not even threaten or scold the couple. They did not ask anything either.

"Sir, you have been called by the inspector to the police station."

"I'll come early in the morning tomorrow." Gopal did not want to go at night, even though he knew that arguing with the policemen was inviting danger. To be arrested at night could be dangerous. His body seemed to swell with fear. He looked at his wife through the faint light of the *tuki*. She had always been a thin woman and now looked even thinner as her face was ashen with fear. Her nose looked more pointed. She just stared at her husband. Gopal pretended that everything was fine to hide his unease before his wife.

"No. You must go with us right now," the police insisted.

"There is no choice but to go with them, even though anything might happen to me."

Though he was mentally prepared to go to the police station, Gopal's legs were not ready to walk. His hands did not lift themselves to put on his clothes. Seeing him dilly-dallying, one of the policemen found his shoes and placed them in front of him.

"I will also go with him," Buddhikala said to the police.

"No, you need not go. It's only up to the police station. He'll surely come back by tomorrow morning."

"The children are here, and if both of us were to go . . ." Gopal looked at his children. His two daughters, aged five and two, were in deep sleep. However, his eight-year-old son, waking up from his sleep, was looking at them quietly.

"Oh. I did not think about the children," Buddhikala backtracked upon hearing her husband. Gopal looked at his children and wife with a sense of deep love. Standing there, he wanted to look at them for an eternity. "How can one trust the police? Who knows whether this might be my last time with my family?" He was becoming weaker. He felt like showering kisses on his children. He felt like embracing his beloved wife, but could not. His heart ached. His eyes were swimming in tears.

"If they don't let me return, goodbye my dear children, goodbye my beloved," he murmured tearfully, but could not verbalize his feelings into audible words. "Be patient. Take care of the children. It won't be dark all the time . . ." he stopped halfway, though the police were pushing him.

"OK, don't worry," said Buddhikala obediently, suppressing her weeping. Tears rolled down her cheeks. She immediately turned to the side and wiped them because she didn't want her husband to see her weeping. "If he is beaten or mistreated, you will not get away with it," she warned as the police left the yard.

"She can keep the home fires burning even in my absence," Gopal thought. His wife's boldness made him proud and confident.

"Now I must go." Gopal said farewell, looking at Buddhikala with his hopeless eyes. He then walked away silently. Buddhikala watched until the glimmering of the torchlight disappeared in the distance. When the light faded, her pain of parting became too much to bear. She ran to her room, embraced her children, and burst into tears.

"He will return tomorrow morning." The words of the policeman echoed in her ears. She trusted the words and waited for the morning, leaving the door open.

Night passed hour by hour and it was ten in the morning, but Buddhikala knew nothing of her husband's whereabouts. No matter how slow a person walked, the distance from the police station to their home was not more than an hour. When her patience had reached its threshold, Buddhikala headed for the police station.

"No one has been brought here. If your husband was arrested, he was probably taken to the next police station," an officer told her.

"Please God, I hope this is true." Buddhikala let out a long sigh. Without delay, she set off for the headquarters. Hurrying like a mad woman and in no time, she had covered a distance that usually took two hours.

"No one has been brought here," she got the same response from the next police station, too. She was tired, and the whole world before her turned dark at once. "Has he been taken straight to the jail then?" Once again her face lit up with the rays of hope.

Hanging on to this hope, she reached the prison to ask about her husband's whereabouts. There, too, she got nothing but disappointment. The possibility of finding him alive faded away. Losing herself in a void, she wandered on the road.

Then she met a lawyer she knew. She narrated the whole story to him.

"The police might have hidden him somewhere, or he might have been transferred to another district. A complaint should be lodged at the court." The lawyer revived her spirits. That day, she returned home with the hope of finding her husband.

"Why didn't our father come home, mother?" the children asked as soon as they saw her. Buddhikala felt her chest pierced, crumbling into pieces. She stood aghast.

"He will come tomorrow," the words unwittingly slipped from her tongue. She could not think fast enough whether it was right or wrong to lie to her children. People in the village talked about Gopal's disappearance the whole day, but nobody brought news of his whereabouts.

In the early morning of the third day, a shepherd completed the story of Gopal's disappearance.

"It happened during the night two days ago while I was sleeping in a cowshed. Below the cowshed, there is an open meadow through which a path goes into the jungle. I noticed something happening as I woke up. Some men with torchlights in their hands were going towards the jungle from that path. *Something fishy is going on there,* I thought, and followed them secretly. I could not see them when they reached the ravine in the jungle. I stopped to listen to them arguing.

"I would rather die holding a gun than be killed defenseless," it was a confident voice speaking, which sounded familiar to me. 'I regret that I did not take the gun.' Someone is being killed there, I concluded. My heartbeat quickened. My hair stood up on the back of my head.

'Take the gun,' someone seemed to be saying sarcastically.

'May the devil take you! May the devil take your chief! My spirit will be baying for blood,' the same voice retorted.

"Meanwhile, I heard the shrill sound of a whistle. Lights glimmered, appearing and disappearing. I heard a rustle of dead leaves coming from a short distance away. Complete silence! Then, the rattle of bullets. Frightened, I ran back and came to my senses only when I reached the cowshed.

'Who was killed? Have they taken the body with them or left it in the jungle?' The overpowering curiosity made me impatient. With the break of day, I released the cattle and took them to the meadow. Then I went towards the ravine in the jungle. I saw blood on the ground, clotted and black. The nearby trees were riddled with bullets and saplings had been trampled. But there was no sign of a dead body. I searched for the body through the entire jungle but could not find it.

"When I was tired of searching, something came to my mind. There is a waterfall below the ravine from where I heard the gunshot. It would be difficult to find even a dead body if someone had fallen from there. No one could go down the ravine. They must certainly have thrown the body there. I hurriedly climbed down. My calculation turned out to be true: I saw the dead body. I trembled with fear. It was Gopal's."

The tragedy spread like wildfire through the village. But Buddhikala had already left for the headquarters. She was walking eagerly, hoping to see her husband in court. The tail of her sari floated in the gently blowing wind.

*****

MAHESHBIKRAMSHAH (1965)

Born in Kalimati of Achham district in far western Nepal, Mahesh Bikram Shah has been serving in the Nepal Police. He is a powerful short story writer, capable of capturing contemporary issues. He started writing from an unusually young age: he was just fourteen when his first story titled *Aama* (Mother) was published. His story collections are *Sataha* (Barterer, 1998), *Sipahiki Swasni* (The Soldier's Wife, 2002), *Afrikan Amigo* (African Amigo, 2003), *Chhapamarko Chhoro* (The Guerilla's Son, 2007), and *Kathmanduma Kamred* (Comrade in Kathmandu, 2009). Shah won the *Madan Puraskar*, a prestigious prize in Nepali literature, for his collection *Chhapamarko Chhoro*, which includes sixteen stories of war and conflict. The stories depict the country's decade-long Maoist-Government war. He has successfully navigated different sides of the conflict and advocated peace in his stories.

In the words of Dr. Govinda Raj Bhattarai, Mahesh Bikram Shah "can smell, see, and sense human sufferings from very close." Shah wrote some of his stories such as *Night Club* and *Pritoriyako Chiso Rat* (The Cold Night of Pretoria) while he was in Mozambique and East Timor serving with Nepal's UN missions. Several of his stories, like *Sipahiki Swasni* and *Badhashalama Buddha* (Buddha in the Slaughterhouse), were written while the country was seething with Maoist rebellion and he was posted in the war-torn regions. "This is the reality I experienced. I am also involved in the armed struggle," he writes. Taken from *Chhapamarko Chhoro*, the present story offers an inside view of a slaughterhouse. The slaughterhouse is a metaphor for those places where violence and lawlessness rule.

Buddha in the Slaughterhouse

He was brought to the slaughterhouse as a captive. He had escaped from there only yesterday. He had been aware that he would be ruthlessly killed if he were caught during his escape. Despite the risk, he freed himself from the dreadful atmosphere of the slaughterhouse and hurled himself out in search of an open sky. It was his misfortune that he was captured while escaping. Hands chained behind his back, he was once again brought to the slaughterhouse where he had diligently performed his special skill as an adept slaughterer for many years.

Based on the gravity of the accusations against the condemned people, their physiognomy, and their class, he used to decide the nature of their death. The slaughterers and their leader would be appeased upon seeing the captive slaughterer's skill at beheading men. The thrust of the sword from his dexterous hands could chop the parts of a human body the same way that a skilled gardener trims the twigs from a rose plant. The disfigured bodies slain by his sword would stagger, crying in pain. The more pain the victims experienced, the more delight would glow on the slaughterer's face. The slaughterer would become drunk with pride upon seeing his contented boss. He had become the best slaughterer around after his many years of experience brutally chopping soft human bodies with his sharp weapons.

He had begun to realize that anyone wishing to be the best should be endowed with cruelty while severing the parts of a human body. Seeing helpless people bowing their heads like he-goats for sacrifice on the *astami* day of Dashain, he would be overwhelmed with excitement. In the world, he had begun to believe, there was nothing as powerful as a weapon. For him a weapon was that magic wand which—without a single threatening word—could easily make servile the accused who boast about themselves.

It was a certain event one day that shook his conviction for the first time since he had started butchering people. From that day forth, he was forced to realize that weapons could not be more powerful than human beings. That day in the slaughterhouse, a youth was silently awaiting his turn. He looked peaceful. He showed no eccentric behavior. No sign of pain or terror manifested in his face. He was calm, unlike the previously condemned victims, who used to plead and beg their slaughterers to spare their lives. Looking at his slaughterer's sword and his blood-smeared body, the youth smiled gently. The slaughterer was slaying the people standing in line, one after the other. Hot fresh blood was dripping on the floor from his sword's blade.

As his turn came, the youth raised his head, stretched his body, and looked straight at his slaughterer. Not a fear of death but a sense of victory over it danced in his eyes. Seeing the youth's bright eyes, the slaughterer trembled with the blood-stained sword in his hand. The youth's eyes expressed not an utmost hatred, but a limitless pity for his slaughterer. The slaughterer's cruel soul shook from deep within when he saw the youth looking at him piteously. This helpless youth, who waited for the fatal blow of the sword, looked normal even in the eleventh hour of his life. His calm complexion and the smile on his lips turned his killer to a coward. Ironically, the slaughterer felt himself like a helpless creature, and this realization shook his heart.

"Executioner, you may destroy me, but you cannot defeat me."

The slaughterer's conviction shook from inside when he heard the youth's voice, calm and mellow. His words went against the slaughterhouse's norms. The youth had openly challenged the activities of the slaughterhouse, which was operating under the illusion that it had been doing philanthropic work by killing people. The youth's open challenge maddened the slaughterer, who had more trust in weapons than human reasoning. In a trance of defeated madness, he violently swung his sword at the youth's neck, beheading him instantly.

The youth's face, though lifeless, smiled at the slaughterer. It occurred to him that the dead youth was saying to him, "Executioner, you couldn't defeat me even after beheading me." In dying, the youth had left his killer mentally half-dead. The slaughterer realized that it was impossible to defeat a man even after beheading him with a single thrust of a sword. The slaughterer's unfeeling mind was shaken by the youth's glowing face, bright eyes, innocent smile, and calm posture. The fact that he could not stand a winner even after killing the youth mortified him.

****

The scene of the slaughterhouse had now changed. The slaughterer, who had earned his name as the best slaughterer by beheading hundreds of men, was now a captive. He was lying on the bloody floor. His hands and feet were shackled with iron chains. In the slaughterhouse, there was a growing mobilization of slaughterers of various levels. The eyes of each new slaughterer were filled with surprise. Seeing them, the captive slaughterer filled with hatred and anger. And yet, indifferent to them all, he recalled the same peaceful, patient, and gentle-faced youth who had brought a turning point in his life. The night's severe physical punishment numbed his body. His throat was dry.

He sensed that he was going to be executed. The simple thought of his death shook his heart. While beheading the others, he had never imagined his own death. He had kicked away countless human heads, but he had not once thought that one day his own head would also be kicked away. An event that he had never dreamed of was going to happen today. As a slaughterer, he had killed many people, and now he himself was going to be slaughtered.

He was chained and carried to the main arena of the slaughterhouse. There he saw naked people with their hands tied, and he offered himself to the cruel hands of death. He was led to the chopping block and there he stood still. His hands and legs were freed from the chains. He was stripped naked and his body was smeared with fresh red blood. He was again being forced to become a bloodthirsty slaughterer. A bloody sword, which he had once used, was thrust in his hands. He took the sword and stood still, perplexed and trembling. He was not brought here to be killed but to kill others.

"You're a slaughterer. Your duty is to kill men. You must behead the enemies!" the roaring sound of the slaughterhouse's leader echoed in his ears.

He stared at the sword that was thrust in his hands. He looked around himself and saw the men bowing their heads like a he-goat. The slaughterer closed his eyes and saw the same youth's calm, exuberant, and gently smiling face peering at him through his own soul.

"Big Boss, men can't be defeated by beheading them," he said out of the blue. He flung the sword away. His voice echoed in the slaughterhouse. The turncoat slaughterer was singing the tune of nonviolence. Defamation of the slaughterhouse! A cruel blow to its norms! The hall was echoing with the shouts of anger and terror.

He was chained again. He was brought to the middle of the slaughterhouse and was tied to the *maulo,* the sacrificial post. This was the place where he used to behead the condemned to train the novice slaughterers in new skills and methods. Alas! Today he was being slaughtered on the same post. A death ceremony was being held. It was being celebrated on the day that the disgruntled members of the slaughterhouse would be butchered for going against its norms. The floors and walls of the slaughterhouse were splattered with red blood. The atmosphere was filled with a cloud of smoke and the smell of burnt flesh.

The leader and his slaughterers, with their blood-smeared-bodies and swords in hand, were standing naked around the *maulo.* They were wearing various kinds of masks. Garlands of human skulls were hanging around their necks. Behind them were the Blood Armies. Some were blowing on shinbones or plucking rib-bones, while the rest were hammering on human skulls. These sounds created a harsh melody—death music. The slaughterer looked at his own death ceremony with innocent eyes. He saw his leader and the slaughterers standing around him, smeared with red blood. He saw the Blood Armies playing the death music from the skeletons. "My death is imminent," he spoke, almost visualizing it. Before dying, he wished to see the slaughterhouse, where he had beheaded many innocent people and made his own life futile.

In the last hour of his life, he wished to visit the slaughterhouse. He looked into a small room where a number of condemned children were staggering with hunger and thirst. His eyes at once fixed on the children who were seized from their parents to make them into future slaughterers or Blood Armies. The slaughterer had taught them that the best ideology in the world was that of the slaughterhouse. To implement this rationale, he had also taught them about various equipment and skills for killing people.

He looked at the large room, adjoined by the children's. Some adults were being taught the principles of the slaughterhouse. A slaughterer was preaching sermons about various strategies of killing people. Nearby, some youths were practicing slaughtering tactics—methods of death punishment—judging on the severity of the accusations against the condemned. The slaughterer regretted his thoughtless involvement in human murder. He was the one who had trained his fellow slaughterers in the brutal strategies of killing.

The training session was becoming harsher and more horrific.

His eyes were fixed on the room from where pathetic cries were resounding. Innocent people of various ages, classes, sexes, and professions were being punished for advocating against the norms of the slaughterhouse. Imprisoned for months, these condemned prisoners were little more than skeletons. The mournful cries coming from their dried throats were making the slaughterhouse's atmosphere appropriate for its activities. The slaughterer was broken seeing the terror-stricken captive's fear of their imminent death.

In front of him were small piles of stacked human skeletons. Pools of blood were all around. Looking at the piles of bones and pools of blood, he thought: 'These bones and this blood won't prove the significance of the slaughterhouse. The future will seek retribution for these bone-piles and blood-pools from these slaughterers and their leader.'

"By all means this slaughterhouse is false, and false are its followers," yelled out the slaughterer.

Hearing his words, a deep silence fell upon the slaughterhouse's death-rejoicing atmosphere. Then, the death music of the Blood Armies began to play; the music grew harsher as if asking for his death.

Now came the final phase of the death celebration—murder. Breaking from the group of the leader and his slaughterers, who were standing around the *maulo*, a slaughterer advanced towards him with a heavy sword. The death music became even more intense, so too did the chorus of the Blood Armies. The captive slaughterer saw the man approaching, lifting the sword.

He now realized the real terror of death, which he had never imagined, not even when he was slaying hundreds of heads. He used to think himself a *death-winner* at others unnatural, untimely, and unjust deaths. Now he had an epiphany that his feeling of victory was nothing more than the madness of an inveterate killer.

"They won't be able to uproot my thoughts of nonviolence even after killing me. They won't defeat me," he thought as the light of this nirvana illuminated his face. The slaughtered youth's peaceful bright face, half-opened eyes, and gently smiling lips flashed before him. The youth's lips began to move and the slaughterer heard his gentle voice, "Hey, follower of nonviolence! You also have Buddha in you. Search for it and find it in yourself. The ultimate truth of this slaughterhouse is to attain Buddhist nirvana."

He felt as if he, too, had attained nirvana. Suddenly, a solemn voice came from his throat—

"I wish to go to the shelter of Buddha. I wish to go to the shelter of religion. I wish to go to the shelter of society."

Suddenly there was silence in the slaughterhouse. "I wish to go to the shelter of Buddha," chanted the turncoat slaughterer in a faint voice at the last hour of his life.

Perplexed is the slaughterhouse, perplexed are its followers, so is the slaughterer standing with the sword in his hands. The words

"I wish to go to the shelter of Buddha" echo louder. These words of truth fill the entire atmosphere. The Blood Armies' lips also begin to flutter. They are surprised to find that this reverberation is quite lively, enchanting, and more pleasing to their ears than that of the death celebration. The leader and his slaughterers are speechless. But a glimpse of their faces indicates that the lively chant is slowly reviving the Buddha inside them.

*****

SHARMILA KHADKA (1966)

Sharmila Khadka (Dahal), born in Dharan in eastern Nepal, writes children's literature. However, she has proved herself talented at writing short stories for readers of all ages. She has published more than half a dozen books of short stories and novels for children. *Samayako Kyanbhasma* (On the Canvas of Time, 2008) is her collection of twenty-four stories. Her children's novels include *Sani* (2003), *Mitratako Mahattwa* (The Importance of Friendship, 2006), *Saniko Sahas* (Sani's Valor, 2005), and *Sinkeko Safalta* (Sinke's Success, 2007). Sharmila was awarded the *Sajha Balsahitya Puraskar* for her first book, *Sani*, a novel based on child psychology. She was also honored with the Excellent Woman Writer's Award (2007), the Gunjan Talent Award (2009), among others.

Sharmila writes psychological stories, in which readers find a detailed picture of female experiences and a thoughtful exploration of human sentiment. In her story writing, Parashu Pradhan notes: "Like the flowing water of a river, there is a stream of consciousness in each of her stories; this is a powerful element for a story." In her stories, Sharmila focuses on the effective presentation of subject matters to jolt reader's minds. The present story, *Sukankya Urf Nilima* (Sukanya, Alias Nilima), is about a high-ranking government officer and a female Maoist fighter. The author presents the officer's point of view and his stream of thought in the story. The officer is psychologically attached to the young girl, who helps take care of him after he is maimed in an attack on the headquarters.

Sukanya, Alias Nilima

I feel the warmth of a woman's exhalation. I wake up. I am unconscious. My eyes open with difficultly, but close again. All my senses are inactive. Slowly I try to take in the information of my surroundings. I find myself so weak that I cannot muster energy to do anything. I again try to mobilize my senses. I lift my right hand, feeling its heaviness, and bring it to her mouth. She is sleeping on my left, touching her plump chest to mine. I feel a ring on her nose. Half of her body tosses with mine. My body is numbed with pain and it feels like somebody else's. I choke as I try to speak. The connection between my heart and mind is gone. My mind is empty. Strength has gone. I am unable to think anything. After a while I give my mind a jolt like something is repeated from a film.

Where am I? Who am I sleeping with? Did I ruin this woman's future in a moment of weakness from the intoxication of a heavy drink? No, up to now I have never ogled at any woman. If so, then who is this woman sleeping with me?

A fuzzy picture of a small house, more like a hut, located in a jungle, comes to my mind. Signaling daybreak, birds are chirping outside. I remember now. I have been posted as a district officer or CDO from Kathmandu to this remote district of western Nepal. I search my memory.

I am here now. Where was I yesterday? What was I doing? I stretch my memory more. All these images coming into my unconscious mind slowly fade away when they are replaced with consciousness. Thousands of sounds start to rattle.

****

"Beware! . . . Fire! . . . Shoot! . . . Surrender! . . . We've captured the headquarters. Save the public houses . . . Adhar! Pratik! Move . . . Stay together in a group . . . *Bang! Bang! Bang! Bang!* Fire! *Bang!*"

All around are gunshots. The sporadic blasts of the bombs rock the houses. The rattle of thousands of guns are producing ear-numbing sounds. Cries, wails, and yells! A fusillade of bullets is falling like hailstones on the rooftops of houses. A while ago, a man was shouting, "Switch off the light!" Shortly afterwards the light goes off. They must have blown out the electric transmitter. A bomb blast rocks the ground. Darkness has enveloped the area, just as a black python devours its prey. The flash of light and the crash of thunder are coming together almost instantaneously.

I am in the CDO quarter. I am just preparing to go to bed. My God! What a deadly war. Never in my life had I witnessed death slow closely. Nevertheless, I had put my life under the sword of Damocles that hung over my head while coming here as the CDO. And yet, I find a great difference between reality and my imagination.

I am very nervous. I drag the telephone to make a phone call. A bullet ricochets off the nearby window. I shrink. I go under the bed. Soon later, I hear the phone ring and take the receiver with difficulty. The deputy superintendent of police speaks from the other end.

"Sir, what shall I do? We're warned to surrender," the frantic voice's words come clearly.

"It's your duty to provide security. Do what you can. We won't survive now," I say frantically.

"Let's not surrender. I have heard that the army is being mobilized!"

"Do whatever you can!"

Then, I go down to the floor below. The families of the peon and the other staff have holed themselves up under the bed downstairs. Battle cries are coming continuously from outside. I am restless. I lay down on the floor. With all are wailing and crying, someone is trying to break the compound gate. I am terrified; my mouth goes dry.

I come out through the back door of my quarters. A huge cliff lies behind it. There is silence below the cliff—no sound, no light. Instantly, I set my mind like a computer and enter the room in search of a rope and do not see one. Near a corner, I see a sari belonging to the peon's wife. I grab it and come out. Outside they are trying to barge through the gate.

I hurriedly tie one end of the sari to a tree and slide down along with it. As I slip down a little, the sari comes untied from the tree. I am wrapped in it and fall down down until I bang with a thud on a narrow pathway. I am injured with wounds and scars all over my body. I do not feel pain, just fear. I don't see a house anywhere. I walk down a little and see a small cottage below a cliff. I again tie the sari on a tree with difficulty and slip down along with it. This time thorns scratch my body. My mental pain easily overcomes my bodily pain. I drag myself to the hut. I see a padlock hanging on its door. I clutch the lock and hang on it. I am not in a condition to stand on my own. Good God! The padlock opens. I fling it and enter. I am assured that nobody is inside. I try to close the door, but I find neither the crossbar nor the bolt of the door. I collapse on the floor after pushing the door closed. I make an effort to rise. What happens next — I can't remember.

****

Now I have regained my consciousness — Is this female body

81

dead or alive? I try to touch it, but no one is there. Is it an illusion or a ghost? Doubt and fear overcome me. I look all around the room. After a while, I see a female body lighting a lamp in a corner. Taking the lamp she sits beside me on a *pirka.* She turns her face away from mine. I do not see her clearly. I move my body to attract her attention and let out an audible sigh. She turns her gaze to look at me. I can read her face — delineated with a little shyness, a little fright, and a little patience.

Slowly it occurs to me that her face is familiar. I look at her with a surprise—"You!"

"Yes, sir . . . I am Sukanya."

Her tranquil face and innocent way of looking lure me. I recall something; Sukanya is one of the most beautiful girls I have ever known. *But why is she here?* I wonder.

"Sir, you might be wondering how I got here. We came here last night to attack the headquarters. I slipped from my friends and entered my mother's house while returning after the attack. I saw you lying on the floor. Initially, I thought it was my mother lying there. But when the torchlight illuminated your face, it was you. Too much blood had flown from your body. I rubbed some cream on you when you were unconscious. I could not lift you up, sir. So I made a bed on the floor and let you sleep. Thinking that you might not regain consciousness due to the chilling cold, I slept with you to give you the warmth of my body . . ." she stammers while uttering the last sentence. Her face glows in shyness in the light of the *tuki* lamp.

****

A rumor that went around my office was that she joined the Maoist fighters a year ago. Before this, she had come to my office to make a citizenship certificate and for official work as well.

However, we got to know each other better when she finally came for her citizenship certificate.

"Sir, I have to make a citizenship certificate for myself. I am working for a health-related NGO. I will be tenured in my job once I get the certificate. Otherwise, after two months, I will have to quit the job," she said.

"A father's recognition is necessary to get the citizenship certificate. Is your father alive or not?" I was speaking with a young girl who was nineteen or twenty.

"Sir, my father is not with us. That's why it is difficult to get the citizenship certificate. Can you tell me what else I can do? I am ready to do whatever it takes. I have heard that it is not difficult to get the citizenship certificate if you are willing to help me!" My morality was alerted when this young country girl said she was ready to offer *whatever* it took. I asked, "What are you saying? What do you mean by *whatever*? Are you asking to get a citizenship certificate without the recognition of a father?" My words were filled with power and pride.

"It's not that, sir! I do not mean that. I said this just because I had heard that the former CDO used to settle any difficult cases. Sir, I will have to quit my job if I do not get the citizenship certificate. My future will be ruined. I'm told that in Kathmandu a mother's citizenship certificate also works to get her daughter's. So I have come to request this favor of you," Sukanya said politely.

This girl is very smart and fearless and truly does have some knowledge of the former CDO as well, I thought. I also thought it not right to argue much with her. I guessed her story: blinded by sexual desire, an officer like me might have seduced her young mother; then, he must have disappeared, leaving her with a child. As a result, the future of this innocent girl has fallen into this present moment.

She waited for my hopefully positive response. "You must know that the law to make a citizenship certificate from a mother's lineage has not been drafted in our country. Though once it is made, there will not be any problem to give you a certificate," I said to her.

She began gasping with sobs, and her shoulders shook. I was bewildered.

In a soothing voice, she said, "Sir, I heard that my father was also an officer like you!"

"Sir, please provide me the citizenship certificate by saying that you are my father."

'Oh, how fearless this girl is. How can she talk like this before a CDO? And how could I be like her father, even if people who see me think my age ten years older than it really is? It must be my bald head that has convinced her of my age,' I thought, but remained silent.

"How is this possible? Tell me. Can a CDO take the illegal way?" I tried to reconcile her argument with mine.

She came to my office two or three more times. She stopped coming when the possibility of getting the citizenship certificate became slim. Later, I came to learn that she had become a Maoist cadre! I had to be wary of her according to my office staff.

****

"Sir, what are you thinking? Now you have recognized me properly, have you?" Her calm voice interrupts my train of thought. I am drawn to the present.

This time she seems fearless, self-respecting, and rational. She has been here, overcoming the fear of death and showed no signs of horror and fear manifesting in her face. She has devoted her precious life to the burning fire of revolution. Why is such a beautiful girl with this tender body wasting her life?

"Sir, you are thinking why and how I became a Maoist cadre, aren't you? Sir, I became a Maoist not out of my own will. I wouldn't have become a Maoist at any cost if I had got my citizenship certificate. I would have been tenured in my job and would have settled there properly, taking care of my old mother. But I had to quit my job soon afterwards and was compelled to stay at home. Then my friends who knew me started suggesting I join the Maoists, saying that our country required revolutionary fighters. I became a Maoist, sir."

"Aren't you scared to play with bombs and bullets?" I asked her.

"Scared!" she exclaimed.

"Our country requires the sacrifice of youths like us. Corrupt and hypocrite landowning exploiters should be rooted out. We cannot manage even one solid meal a day despite working day and night. We have nothing while they have had a luxurious life. We have to make a prosperous new Nepal. For this we need to revolt. Sir, the exploited class should be uplifted, according to Mao's theory." She seems to be recalling something.

I want to tell her the many weaknesses of her party, but the pain of my body does not let me. She seems to be highly influenced by her party policy.

My whole body aches. I breathe a sigh of pain, "Urgh."

Then she says, "Sir, you are suffering from a severe pain. I will get you a painkiller."

She takes out medicine from some corner of the room

and gives it to me with a glass of water. I can't move one of my legs. There are bruises all over my body. My body starts to ache severely. I notice that she has applied the medicine after cleaning my wounds. I realize it now.

My eyes are fixed on her blouse and sari. I translate my eagerness into words. "You have been to attack the headquarters, but is this the blouse and sari?"

"These belong to my mother. I have hidden my combat uniform. I feared that it would be risky if I wore them now."

I realize that this girl has become very smart. How quickly can she understand the thoughts in another's mind? Why is she putting her life at risk for me? Who is she to me anyway? Why is she showing such generosity?

"Sir, I have studied psychology with the party and taken counseling training since I am able to read. So I can easily guess what you are thinking. Sir, you might be thinking why I am taking such a risk. We also have humanity, even if we are very cruel at the moment. We also have feelings. I can't go leaving you alone in this condition. Sir, we are as insignificant as gnats to you. I have thought that our life is meaningless, but yours is not. You have many hopes that keep on following you, but in my case I have no guarantee for my own life, nor any value. Nor do I have hopes for a future. Later, I came to know that my mother, too, had left me alone."

She looks thoughtful.

I am impatient hearing such things from a beautiful girl. The girl with such a beautiful body and this height of intelligence surprises me. If only she got the opportunity, she could keep the world under her authority. But the plight of the Nepali people is that many such beautiful tender hands are playing with bombs and bullets. So many nubile girls like Sukanya are exchanging their dreams of a brighter future for revolution. They have stifled their happiness, desires and future deep in their hearts.

It is not yet broad daylight outside while we are talking. She enters the room fetching a pitcher of water. She makes a fire in the hearth in a corner and heats the water. She brings maize from somewhere and starts to heat it. Now there is daylight outside. The corn kernels are popping in the *handi*. In my mind, too, various positive and negative ideas burst like the popping corn.

I learned many things about life from her company. We are human beings of two opposite sexes, who follow two opposite ideals. I am one of the male employees working on behalf of the government to provide security for the people; whereas, she is a female guerilla, fighting to topple the government with a revolt. She can challenge death, whereas, I am a coward who escapes it. I have many hopes, beliefs, and desires, which I have been plucking from this beautiful world, while she has been trading her rosy future for bombs and bullets, leading a hopeless miserable present. The present moment and this incident make me emotional and agitated. My writing skills, which were dormant, become alert. Humanity staggers. I become serious and sensitive. I determine to verbalize this unimaginable moment.

"Sir . . . ," she breaks the silence, "I will send word so that some men will come to retrieve you. I myself could take you when night falls but your health might worsen by that time. Therefore, I will make my way, telling someone to take you, sir."

She starts to pack her things while crunching on the maize. I also take a little bit of it. Soon she scribbles something on a piece of paper and steals a glimpse of my face. Becoming serious and sensitive, she says, "Sir, do not forget me if you see me somewhere! Remember me if you hear or read the name Nilima. I hope you recover soon. I will be on my way. After sometime, some men will come to take you. Do not tell anyone anything about me."

Her words make me worried and thoughtful. On the one hand, she is at risk, while on the other my health is getting worse. I speak with difficulty—

"Do not go, Sukanya. Surrender! I will speak on your behalf."

She says patiently, "Sir, it's too late. All my roads of returning have been blocked. My soul will not get peace even if I surrender. It is against our party policy. So, I must go. I do not fear death." She goes out, taking a small bundle that could be her uniform. Still lying on the bed, I just watch her go.

*****

ROSHANTHAPA 'NEERAV' (1967)

Roshan Thapa 'Neerav,' born and brought up in Kathmandu, is a short-fiction writer, novelist, poet, and editor. His first story was *Aantarik Katha* (The Internal Story). His story collections are *Antahin Yuddha* (The Endless War, 2000) and *Tesro Bishwa Yuddha* (Third World War, 2005). His novels are *Pratyek Shrawankumar Arthat Yuddha* (Every Shrawankumar or War, 2007), *Prasthantar* (Different Exit, 2008), and *Swapnasahar* (Dream City, 2009). An editor of more than two-dozen literary books and magazines, Roshan is associated with the Nepali Fiction Society and the literary magazines *Samakalin Sahitya* and *Tanneri Dot Com*. He has solidified his position in story writing and poetry upon receiving various honors and prizes, such as the first prizes in both the Guruprasad Mainali Memorial Story Competition and the National Poem Competition.

Roshan's stories are experimental; he plays with technique. His many stories, idiosyncratic in style, are the sketches of an imaginative reconstruction of reality. Regarding his story writing, Dr. Govinda Raj Bhattarai and Bishnubibhu Ghimire observe: "Neerav, who has the experience of creative writing and editing, writes good, striking, and experimental stories." He shows the evils of the present world, the suffering of men, and their longing for their homeland. "There is man, there is suffering, and there is a place and time in my stories. The style is my own. While presenting them, I never run away from man," Roshan says. His story *Asahya* (Unbearable) is written in verse and is about a youth who returns home after several years only to find that everything he knew is ruined. In the story, the prodigal son relentlessly flits from one scene to the other, and this rapidity of scene change makes the readers feel as if they are flicking through the channels of a television. The story has an unspecified setting in a war-torn region during the decade-long Maoist-Government war in Nepal.

Unbearable

The settlement slumbers guiltlessly under a blanket of terror.

Why the place looks so terrifying -- I do not know.

My curiosity has grown to find the reason, but the terror is so extreme that it is as fearsome as two Hindu devils: *Madhu* and *Kaitabh.*

I have just returned home.

After almost twelve years and eight months.

I have come after many years of postponing my duty to take responsibility for the family.

Yes, I have been here. But I had never imagined that the settlement would be harboring the fear and silence of a graveyard.

Reaching home, I look around. Oh, what on earth do I see? My home, which I left twelve years and eight months ago, is not here. The entire settlement is not here either. The places where homes had been are full of debris.

What happened? Where is my home?

Where are my father and mother? And Shanti, my sister?

Where have the neighbours gone?

I look around, shell-shocked.

The settlement and the village slumber under the shroud of silence far and wide.

I was miles away, but there were frequent exchanges of letters and messages during the years. Father would write letters about home. I began to worry when his letters stopped coming six months ago. However, indifferent to all doubts and rumors, I have returned home, full of hope.

Home/settlement/village.

Greenery/hills/flowers/waterfalls/brooks/birds.

And my beloved, my partner Rakshya.

Where? Where have these reasons for my living gone?

I see them nowhere.

To whom should I cry for help? To whom should I plead?

I see only rubble and ashes all over the settlement.

How did this come to be? Who caused it?

It must have been a great surprise. Not only my home, but the whole village has been reduced to a pile of ashes. More than being surprised, I lose myself in a whirlpool of terror.

Is it that the news about this village reduced to a dust has been shrouded in mystery? Or what?

How could anyone overlook such a terrible event?

I am both shocked and surprised.

Surprised in the sense that at least someone in the village

should have known of the disaster, or at least it should have been in the news. But, why didn't it appear in the news?

And shocked? My family and neighborhood have become the victims of such mystery and destruction, and the settlement has turned into a truly terrifying place. I can neither stop nor run away from here. I have returned from the city with the thought of seeing my sister marry, and seeing my beloved.

Rakshya. My beloved.

She comes into my mind and goes, like a scene from a film.

Our love. That ecstasy. That romance.

A gust of memories comes to my mind and flies away.

The gap in our love had been so long that we almost did not know each other.

My beloved! Where could my beloved be?

I walk on.

With terror and fear following me.

The more I walk the more hellish scenes of the village I see.

Even the silence looms large, becoming unbearable.

Ashes all around! There are no houses!

Only rubble and remnants!

Am I sleepwalking? I pinch myself, but it proves true: I am walking awake. It is as true as the demolished village. What is the reason behind this deadly silence, like a settlement swept away by a landslide, or a society reduced to ashes by a fire in a flash? Which devil came and ravaged the area, spewing a huge ball of fire?

One after the other, fables and anecdotes come to my mind, but not the kind of fable with a devil character who can turn an entire village to rubble and barren land.

I see no bodies.

At least there should have been a body. There are none.

There are only piles of ashes.

Dancing images of my home, my young sister's agility, and my love for my parents glimmer in my eyes. My beloved, sitting at the top of a hill requesting that I pluck a rhododendron to put in her hair, a blush of love spreading on her cheeks, becoming passionate, pulling her in my embrace for a kiss, she pushing me into the crystal water of the brook, me falling in the water and she giggling. The azure sky smiling, the *danphe* bird dancing, and the gentle breeze whispering—many kaleidoscopic images come to my mind, causing my eyes to film over with tears.

I wipe away the tears. My heart aches.

A flood of memories overwhelms me with anguish.

The terror again rises and starts to chase me.

I run.

Wildly.

Silence. Deserted. Alien.

All around.

The temple is no more.

My God! The temple is also completely demolished.

The old district palaces are damaged to their foundations.

I look towards the brook—blood red.

What is it? Who did this?

Was it a bomb? Or a gun?

Or some other weapon?

Was it a storm? Or fire?

Or some other disaster?

When did the disaster strike this settlement, this village? Why did it strike? And how?

My home. My settlement. My village.

My home. My family. My beloved.

Where to search for them now? Maybe after going a short distance—I come across a human figure, naked.

I run. Closer and closer.

A naked body. A young woman's.

Her hair is long.

Lying face down.

Naked from head to toe.

A white body full of welts and bruises, bitten by teeth, scratched by claws, burned by fire.

Wounds are all over.

Who is she?

Amidst the deadly silence, emptiness, and ruins, only one remnant is found, and that too is a corpse.

The remnant of a human.

Getting something is better than nothing.

But who is she?

I turn her over. I look.

Oh, God!

My sister. Shanti. Sister. Lord—a ghastly sight. Both her breasts have been cut off.

Who did this?

What vile and violent animal caused this?

What reply can a dead body give?

I begin to shake. No sound comes from the body.

The body, covered with welts and bruises, terror and hate written in the eyes.

I want to cry, but can't.

Who did this to you, sister?

Alas/tragedy/disaster/what shall I do?

I take off my jacket and cover her dead body.

The tragedy does not stop me.

It makes me run. I run.

Farther and faster.

I come across another human figure. I storm towards it.

It feels like the figure is coming towards me, closer and closer.

With a growing speed, I reach close.

I look and this, too, is a female body, naked.

Lying prostrate on the ground, completely naked.

A similar white body.

Marks are similar. Wounds are similar.

Wounds of teeth, fingernails, and knives.

Clotted blood has formed around her wounds.

I turn the dead body over.

And I see . . . ! Large wounds and marks of rape all over her body.

Oh God! Her genitals have been stabbed with a sharp weapon.

As I observe the body up close . . . !

Oh, God—my love—my beloved—Rakshya!

Now I feel the world around me spinning.

I become speechless though I have many questions.

I find her eyes emanating limitless pain, endless waiting, and unbearable agony.

Now I am completely senseless. I am racked by the unbearable pain.

I cannot stomach this.

I take off the rest of my clothes and cover her naked body.

My beloved . . . Dear God!

Again I start to run faster and faster.

Driven by a dizzying feeling. Driven by an intolerable situation.

Like a person who runs despite the anguish of a wound.

Far and wide I run.

Fear/mystery/terror.

All chasing me.

Now I see the corpses of women at every mile.

Then I see ghastly sights of children as I reach a little farther.

Somebody with amputated hands. Somebody's eyes gouged.

Somebody with a severed tongue. Somebody's genitals cleft.

Alas—what kind of barbarism is this?

What a time! What a scene!

I am completely mute. I cannot utter a single word.

I just run, run, and run, taking the unbearable pain inside me.

And then I begin to see the sporadic figures of middle-aged women, alive.

Curiosity overpowers me.

I attempt to ask but my voice won't come, I don't know how and why. My tongue is tied.

I want to speak, but words cannot be uttered.

I want to ask, but I cannot ask.

I want to cry, but I cannot cry.

I want to stop, but I cannot stop.

And I notice that all the women are mute and motionless, shaking with fear and terror.

Lips tight, eyes blind.

None of them utters a single word.

Not knowing what to do, I continue running faster.

Where? Towards the questions?

Towards the answers? Towards the curiosities?

I don't know my destination.

The only thing I know is I am running, chased by terror, keeping its distance behind me at all times.

Now when shall I have a clean city, a clean time, a clean road? This, which has been my dream for such a long time, is now lost.

The cry of these innocent women for help and their pleading for the right to live echoes in my heart.

Now I wander constantly for the rights of those victimized women. With unbearable responsibilities, I am running in search of murderers.

My goal has not yet been achieved.

*****

RAJKUMARDIKPAL (1972)

Rajkumar Dikpal, born in Dhankuta, a hilly district in eastern Nepal, is the pen name of Rajkumar Subba. He specializes in teaching, journalism, and literature, and works as a senior news correspondent for *The Annapurna Post*, a national daily newspaper. Having earned a master's degree in journalism, Dikpal shows great potential in both journalism and literature. *Aatankako Chhayamuni* (Under the Shadow of Terror, 2007) is his collection of fourteen short stories on a variety of issues and events in Nepal. Dikpal is affiliated with the Federation of Nepalese Journalists (FNJ), the International Federation of Journalists (IFJ), the Association of Nepalese Indigenous Journalists (ANIJ), and the Education Journalists' Group (EJG).

Rajkumar Dikpal's stories are heart wrenching. They show human miseries and the ultimate height of tragedy caused by war or other social ills. Regarding his story writing, Narayan Dhakal notes: "Dikpal's stories are important to depict a powerful canvas of the effects of war." Dikpal, who has a deft hand for realistically presenting events, much like journalistic reporting, says that his stories are the shadows of his surroundings. The present story *Liwang, 2063* (Liwang, 2006), taken from his collection *Aatankako Chhayamuni,* presents a realistic and harrowing picture of an old woman whose son has gone missing after a group of government gunmen steal him away from his house one night before the backdrop of Maoist-Government war in Nepal. Through the passage of time, the story contrasts a changed picture of Liwang with the unchanged and unimproved condition of the victimized woman, who keeps anxiously waiting for her son's safe return.

Liwang, 2006

It is yet to snow on the ridge of Dharampani highland. The elevated land is barren. After the snowfall, it does not melt away until the beginning of the summer season. The visitors, who come first to Liwang during the winter, take it for a mountain. A gust of cold air strikes directly at its heart. Besides this, a late sunrise and an early sunset are Liwang's special features.

I am in Liwang as a volunteer for an NGO working to reconstruct the Rolpa district. The cold has grown. For several weeks, after my morning tea, I have been strolling in Tundikhel basking in the sunrays. I regularly see a puzzling scene. I find that an old woman also comes to Tundikhel. At first I think that she is there to sunbathe like me, but to my surprise, she keeps staring at the distant Gwarpa Hill instead of relaxing in the sun. The old woman does not leave until the dim rays of the sun bid farewell to Dharampani highland. Before I return to my residence, I hear her muttering something, but I can't understand her words.

I want to ask the woman about her business at Tundikhel. I want to know her mystery. What might she be looking for on Gwarpa and its surrounding hills—Mangliwang, Jangkot, and Bhulumdhara? My curiosity finally reaches its extreme.

"Mother, why are you looking at this?" one day, when I cannot suppress my curiosity, I go close to her and muster my courage to ask.

"Purnaman?"

She slowly turns her eyes from Gwarpa hill and looks at me. "Are you not Purnaman?" Again she turns towards the hill.

I am surprised. The question *'Who is Purnaman, mother?'* almost slips from my lips, but I cannot ask her.

My office is near Tundikhel. Looking through the window of my office and seeing the woman, standing and staring like a statue, have become my second job.

"Hello, sir. Why are you following that old woman?" my boss, Shyamsundar, asks me one day. I explain my curiosity about her to him, "Sir, who is that old woman? Why does she always look at the surrounding hills? And who is that Purnaman she speaks of?"

"People said her son disappeared after the crossfire six years ago and she fell apart after that."

My boss tries to dismiss my curiosity with a succinct reply, but my desire to know more takes over. "Where has her son disappeared, sir?" I ask.

"Mr. Raj! How could I possibly know all this? Go and ask her daughter yourself. She is running a small tea shop at Peepalchautari, a little farther from here."

I feel relief even with the grudging reply of my boss. I reach Peeplechautari. There I see a signboard reading *Jaljala* Hotel right above the door of a small hotel. I decide to dine there from that day on.

In the course of having my meals there, I learn that the old woman's name is Dilsara Ghartimagar, age sixty-two.

****

The face of Liwang has changed now. This place remains awake till late at night while it used to live under the suffocation of curfew-clamped nights beginning at five o'clock. The Liwang bazaar has started to crawl with youths who have rejoined the fashion of rap and hip-hop. The rooftops of private houses, which were used as sentry posts by the police and the army, have started to be fluted with concrete columns. Moreover, new construction sites begin to appear on the roadsides.

Once thrashed by the Maoists, then by the police, Chitra Bahadur Punmagar, a retired soldier from the Indian Army, occasionally comes drunk to Tundikhel from his house in Jankot and shows off his martial arts. "I need not give the second blow to whoever comes to fight me!" he shouts in a tipsy mood.

The life of Liwang burgeons day by day, but Dilsara Ghartimagar lives the same unchanged, hopeless life. She drowns in sorrow after the government gunmen abducted her son, Purnaman, from their home in Iriwang, under the pretext of making an inquiry. Like the flowing water of Dhangsikhola, tears roll down her cheeks, but Purnaman's condition is as much unknown as the amount of water flowing downstream.

"Mother's condition worsened after her son, whom she had reared with difficulty and great care, did not return, sir," her daughter Bainsamali tells me one day while serving me a meal.

She said, "Our family was not rich, yet it was living happily. Tragedy first struck us when our father died after he had fallen off a cliff. At that time, Purnaman was only a toddler. The responsibility of caring for him, and a hope she had pinned on him, healed mother's wound. I came to live in Liwang after my marriage. My husband has gone to India for employment. Since then I have been running the *Jaljala* Hotel to support my family."

"After the beginning of the war, some joined in while others left the village to save their lives. But Purnaman did not leave his home. 'I haven't done anything wrong. Why should I be afraid?' he would say. However, constant pressure continued to weigh on him. A group of people saying, 'Come with us,' kept descending on his house. At first Purnaman rejected them outright, 'I won't go.' Then he resisted going with them by making up different excuses. Finally, he made various fake promises when the pressure grew too strong.

"Now what will you do, Purnaman?" Mother asked him one evening while the two were talking in the dim light of a *tuki* lamp after they had eaten *dhindo*.

"Tell me what to do, Mother," he asked, idealess. Then, amplifying his voice in a flurry of excitement as if a sudden idea had flashed in his mind, Purnaman spoke, "Mother, I would rather go to a foreign country."

"You would like to go where your brother-in-law has gone?" mother asked.

"No! Why do you say that, Mother? What's the use of going to India? If I have to go, I should choose a better country," Purnima said boldly.

"You go, leaving me alone then?" Mother asked, "And you haven't married, either."

"What are you saying, mother?" Purnaman asked, adding, "First, I will earn money, then I will marry with the fanfare of a traditional musical band. Every cloud has a silver lining, doesn't it mother?" Mother thought that her son's plan was considerable. She seemed to be remembering something for a while. Then she brought her hands towards her ears and said, "Take these and sell them to get a passport." She placed her gold earrings in Purnaman's hand.

"If my brother headed straight for Liwang from his village in Iriwang to make his passport, the rebels would know what he was doing and he would have to explain himself. That was why he made a plan to take the path to Holeri and then reach Ghorahi under the pretext that he had some work there. From Ghorahi, he would then go to Liwang, having walked all the way through Bhaluwang.

"As the mother and brother were about to put out the *tuki* lamp after their plan was fixed, somebody knocked on the door.

"Who is it?" Purnaman asked.

"It's us, Mr. Purna. Please open the door."

Brother opened the door after he thought the voice he had heard was familiar. They were in fact his friends who had entered the jungle with guns.

"We are twenty-two. Cook a meal for us or rather—provide us the ingredients. Our friends will cook for themselves," group commander Comrade Prabesh spoke after the door was opened.

Mother brought some ground corn to cook cornmeal for them. Purnaman and Comrade Prabesh began to talk while the rest joined in cooking.

"Mr. Purna, we need a person like you," he said.

Brother had already guessed that Comrade Prabesh was going to say this. He said, "I have to go to Dang tomorrow. It's urgent, but I will go with you once returning from there." Purnaman was thinking something different though: "Then you will see how I give you the slip and flee abroad."

At first Comrade Prabesh doubted Purnaman's request; however, he nodded his head in agreement after some time. A rooster heralded morning with its cock-a-doodle-doo shortly after they had eaten and slept and the group went on their way.

An hour later, a group of government gunmen picketed the house. "Where have they gone? You give shelter to the Maoists, eh? Boys, arrest him!" exploded their commander.

Two gunmen grabbed Purnaman. "Where are you taking him? Tell me!" Mother protested.

"It's not serious, Mother. Nothing will happen to your son. We will send him back after an inquiry," one of them spoke diplomatically.

Many days passed since they took my brother, but they never brought him back. As the days passed, mother also stopped crying. I have been taking care of her ever since. I took her with me from the village after her condition worsened.

****

While recounting the tale about her brother's disappearance, Bainsamali begins to sob. As I eat my meal, tears well up in my eyes, too. The reason for Dilsara's regular arrival at Tundikhel becomes clear to me now.

Now it's time for me to leave Rolpa, but the forlorn mother has not yet stopped staring at Gwarpa Hill. Before I return to Kathmandu, Bainsamali says, giving me Purnaman's photo, "If my brother is found somewhere, don't forget to inform us, OK sir?"

From the bus park, I catch a bus to Kathmandu. It leaves at eleven in the morning. I get my seat. After looking at Purnaman's photo, I open the window to look at Tundikhel. Dilsara still keeps on staring at Gwarpa Hill.

*****

NAWASILWAL (1973)

Born and brought up in Godawari of Lalitpur, Nawa Silwal is involved in law enforcement as a police officer. He has published a dozen books on law and order management, human rights, traffic management, crime investigation, scientific management, and air pollution. As a staff member of the United Nations Organization, Silwal has traveled to Mozambique, Ivory Coast, Liberia, Timor and other countries in western and southern Africa. In addition to this, he is involved in several literary creations and his two collections of short stories have been published to date. They are *Aasthako Pahad* (The Mountain of Faith, 2006), a collection of twenty stories, and *Sabdabihin Aawajharu* (The Sounds without Words, 2010).

In his stories, Nawa Silwal presents the absurd side of human life and advocates humanity. For this purpose, he foregrounds the plight of security personnel, rebels, ordinary people, and the injured victims of the Maoist-Government war. "The stories of Nawal Silwal," writes Prof. Mohanraj Sharma, "are capable of drawing a realistic picture of present day absurdities." Silwal successfully weaves the real characters of society into his stories when he writes in an effort to share his feelings and experiences. Taken from his collection *Aasthako Pahad*, the following story, *Kaidi* (The Prisoner), presents the piteous condition of a soldier who has fallen into the hands of rebels. The story protests war through a striking monologue of an old woman. The surprise ending raises hope for humanity.

The Prisoner

The sounds of bombs and bullets had unleashed a terror on the bank of the Gandaki River. The number of people being killed was growing with the deepening night. The rebels had intensified their attack on security forces. The silence and darkness of the night were appearing, full of fear. It was a war of one Nepali killing another. The war, which led to terrible explosions and demonstrated the valuelessness of human life, seemed in one sense bound to eliminate human civilization in the name of seeking freedom. Such a war is fought in the place where the importance of humanity is feeble, the meaning of human life is nil, and where such annihilations take place every now and then.

The rebels took over the town with their night-long attack. As the dawn turned night into daylight, streets and fields were seen awash with corpses. The still-smoldering police offices and government buildings were emanating fear.

"Sir, I've arrested a government soldier," a rebel reported to his commander.

"All right. Good! Bring him here!" the commander ordered.

The rebels tied the soldier's hands and led him with them towards the jungle. He looked somber. The fresh recollection of the night's clash and of his friends falling prey to bombs and bullets shook his heart from inside. He was not happy despite being unharmed from the night's fierce attack. The event had a deadening effect on him; his senses had been numbed. He had lost his sense of existence. With no hope for the future, his complete being had been narrowed into the role of a mere prisoner.

Following the rebel's order, the prisoner stopped at times while walking. He knew nothing about his journey or its destination. He was now a mere captive who waited for the rebel's small decisions.

The sun rose. There was no movement in the middle of the jungle. The sense of death was pervasive around them. Birds and animals seemed not to exist. The prisoner was journeying towards his graveyard.

The commander called his two rebels towards him and muttered something. They nodded their heads and came back.

"Hey, Mercenary, you have fallen into a trap," a rebel vented his anger.

"All right, I'm ready," he said to himself and remained calm.

The two rebels were probably told to take him to a certain destination.

"Ah, his eyes express hatred against us. Do I finish him right now?" a rebel roared.

"No. He is our captive. Don't do anything to him. He will meet his fate as the time comes," the other rebel said calmly.

The two rebels were probably told to take him to a place where he would be killed.

"Comrade Mangal, I will take a rest for a while. Keep your vigilant eyes on him. We will continue when the sun sets."

"All right, Comrade Himal!" the other rebel nodded his head. The heat in the middle of the jungle suffocated them. The moments of dead air had made the jungle atmosphere irritating.

Comrade Mangal started to snore, lolling his head on his knee. This man, the prisoner thought, is somehow prudent and practical. In the oblivion of his meaningless life, he tried to study the two men who were the deciders of his fate.

It occurred to the prisoner that the rebels had been accustomed to hatred and passion. Maybe they found meaning only in fighting and finishing people off. It seemed that the rebellion and hatred had manifested into their words and feelings. The prisoner, however, was not interested in knowing whether their hatred was towards their own land or government soldiers like him. His restrained hands were suffering from an increasing pain. He did not say anything, however. He was also a hardened man like the rebels. The situation he was facing made him cruel and rigid. Waves of pain surged through his body, but he hid his discomfort and remained calm.

He looked at the rebel who was guarding him. The guard, who was wearing a worn out combat dress, also collapsed on the ground. A small pistol hung from his waist. His body was lean and weak, but cruelty was obvious on his face. This could have been his obligation or physical characteristics, or a mask he wore to hide his true nature. He might not have been in the position to revolt within himself.

The rebel, who was snoring from the ground, seemed hardened to his beliefs, but sensitive.

The daylight was fading. The captive was attempting to blot out the memories of his family and his past. He did not want to weaken himself by recollecting the things related to his past.

'They're surely going to kill me. I could just be waiting for a short time,' the prisoner thought. *The wait for death was in front of him, growing terrible. 'Waiting for death in fact is more painful than dying itself,'* he thought further.

Comrade Mangal stood up. "Let's get on our way. We have

to reach the Otar village before night." Their journey continued.

The captive was between them. Comrade Mangal led the way while comrade Himal walked behind the captive, catching one end of the rope while the other was tied to the captive's hand.

They proceeded towards their destination.

"Where are you taking me?" spoke the prisoner out of the blue.

The rebels only stared at him. They had no reply. The atmosphere was pained.

The continuous rustling of their footsteps coming from dry leaves was pervasive around them. "Why, why don't you speak? You're taking me to be killed, aren't you?" the prisoner asked, raising his voice.

Comrade Himal halted at once. He looked at his captive. He had no reply. His eyes were full of complexities.

"We're going to hand you over to the Kangaroo Court. Whatever it is—life or death—you'll get it there," said Comrade Himal, who was holding one end of the rope tying back the prisoner's hands. His reply sounded plain.

Their journey went on. The rebels didn't speak; perhaps they spoke far less. They knew the fate of the captive.

"They can give only death to a soldier who has killed their friends. They're surely going to execute me," the prisoner murmured.

He realized that enough obstacles were before him. He could neither escape, nor attack the rebels. He was moving ahead with the current of time to meet his death while the rebels were committed to pushing him into its mouth. What an unnatural situation! What a dilemma! What an obligation! He was walking, silent. The rustle of dry leaves arising from the rebel's footsteps struck his eardrums as though it was death music.

The three men reached a house in the Otar village before it was pitch dark. There in the house an old woman began to cook for them. They were tired after their day-long walk. The woman, nearing her old age, looked curious. She tried to peer at the prisoner's face with the help of the dim light of a *tuki* lamp.

"Who is he, Son?" she asked a rebel.

"He is our enemy, Mother. We brought him here after catching him," the reply was simple.

"Where are you taking him then?"

"To file a complaint in the Kangaroo Court."

"Alas!" Pity grew in her. "So, they are going to kill this boy, too! I haven't heard the Kangaroo Court forgiving one of its enemies."

Peering at his face in the dim light, she began to recall something.

"Oh! This boy has a fair complexion like my son's. The sinners are going to kill him, too. The old-age support for a mother's life is being seized. Tch tch tch . . ." she muttered in sadness. She seemed to be accustomed to the rebel's activities. She brought the *roti* and *gundruk* soup for her three guests. The two rebels began to eat the *roti*.

The hot steam coming from the bowls was invisible in the darkness.

The captive soldier tried to find an image of his mother in the old woman. Who will take care of his destitute mother, who had been living on her son's earning in a remote village of Gulmi district? He became agitated. His own life had turned cruel.

The old woman squatted, coming close to him. "Why aren't you eating? Eat, Son. Tomorrow morning you will not be given anything to eat. They will call the court early in the morning at the Tikure Chautari and the sinners will behead you," she exclaimed.

The atmosphere was terrible. The rebels were satisfying their hunger with the pieces of *roti*.

"Maila, free his hands at least for eating!" the woman requested Comrade Mangal.

"No, we shouldn't. He'll escape," Comrade Himal roared, which was perhaps an effort to conceal the weakness of his gaunt body. There was again the silence of death. The dim light of the *tuki* lamp seemed to be spewing fear.

The old woman put a piece of bread into the prisoner's mouth. He saw in her a mirror image of his mother. He had no desire to eat. He, however, could not deny her kindness. He gulped the *roti* and the *gundruk* that she fed him.

"Don't show mercy to our enemy, Mother," exploded the lean rebel.

The old woman shrank and stood abruptly. She began to sob. "Kill me instead, but free him. He is also the son of a Nepali. He is also your brother, not an enemy. Don't kill him," she choked while she was crying. The night deepened. The three people passed during the night, hour after hour, while waiting for the morning. The two rebels, their captive in the house of a remote village, and an old woman trying to play her role amidst the fear and terror of great rivalry! This scene reflected the country's deadlock as such situations were common all across the country.

It was early morning. A lean boy of ten or eleven, wearing a tattered cap, his toes sticking out of his shabby shoes, arrived. The rebels told him to deliver the message that the court be called at eight o'clock and the boy left.

The prisoner looked at the sun, which was rising above in the horizon. *'The last sun of my life is rising,'* he thought. He wanted to harden himself and hate his own body. He did not pray for God. *'God is powerless,'* he murmured. "If God were almighty, why would such massacres have taken place? Why would exploiters be exploiting and the rebels be fighting the rebellion? God is powerless, quite powerless." A pity for God's feeble existence came to him.

The court began amidst the crowd of people who were bunching together to listen to a decision. The judge sat on an old chair at the platform. He was trying to show himself gentle and unbiased.

The captive soldier caught a familiar face amongst the rebels standing in a line. He could not believe his eyes. It was his sister, Chameli, who had gone missing from home six months ago. She was weeping loudly, shedding tears, while a rebel nearby was warning her to be quiet.

Charges against the prisoner were submitted to the judge. The prisoner spoke no word in his defense. The court did not take long to make its decision. The judge coldly announced his execution. The crowd mourned.

"Do you have any last words?" asked the judge.

"I wish to be killed in the jungle, away from this crowd," begged the prisoner.

"Well, execute him the way he has demanded," the judge ordered.

Comrade Himal and Mangal took him to the jungle.

The prisoner looked at his sister and cried, "Chameli, take care of mother."

Bursting into tears, Chameli ran to embrace her brother.

"You'd better kill me, but leave my brother," she pleaded, turning first to the rebels, then to the judge. "My mother will die of hunger. Kill me. Let my brother free." She began to cry uncontrollably, her worn out combat dress showered with her own tears. The atmosphere seemed to reflect the moment—someone was crying over a relative's dead body, with other mourners silently expressing their condolences. No one showed pity for the girl's heartrending cry. It seemed that love and mercy did not dwell in the hearts of the people living in the village where the majority were rebels.

The judge looked around and stood straight from his chair in an authoritative manner. Then he gestured to the rebels that the prisoner be taken to the jungle.

The rebels Himal and Mangal led the prisoner away from the crowd. There was no one who could protest. The crowd was mute with no sound or reaction, like a mass of dead bodies. They were unfeeling. Chameli's sorrowful cry broke the silence and reached far and wide — as far as the edge of the jungle.

The rebels reached a hillock in the middle of the dense jungle and stopped. The captive also stopped after his hands felt a jerk of the rope. He looked somber, as if the flow of his life had come to a standstill. In that part of the jungle, time also seemed to be stopping.

Comrade Mangal heaved a deep sigh, and it seemed as though he wanted to revolt. 'What type of rebellion is this where people are killed? This has only created a wave of killing by our own hands. This should be stopped,' he thought. 'Can't there be a rebellion without murder and violence?'

Comrade Mangal controlled himself and asked for the pistol hanging from Comrade Himal's waist. Himal took the pistol out of his holster and handed it to Mangal.

"Comrade Himal! Untie the captive's hands," Comrade Mangal exclaimed in semi-command. He saw the captive's swelling hands. Comrade Mangal pointed the pistol at him. The prisoner looked above at the sky, remembered his old mother, and asked her to forgive him. "All right, shoot," he shouted, trying to be strong.

Comrade Mangal pointed his pistol at the prisoner. He waited for a short time, fired two shots in the air and hurried to embrace the prisoner. "Brother, you are freed, go on your way," Comrade Mangal said.

Comrade Himal stood, aghast.

"Comrade, what have you done to the court verdict?" he exclaimed.

"Shh!" comrade Mangal signaled Himal not to speak with a gesture of his index finger. Their eyes brimmed with the tears of happiness. A faint smile surged on their lips. The rebels quietly departed their separate ways. The captive collapsed on the ground. He had a rigid heart, but his dry eyes also began to well up and tear-drops rolled unwittingly. He did not know whether the tears were of happiness or misery . . .

*****

HOMSHANKARBASTOLA
(1974)

Homshankar Bastola, born in Okhaldhunga district in eastern Nepal, is an aspiring short story writer. His two short story collections, *Aansuka Jharanaharu* (Falls of Tears, 2001) and *Bandukko Chhaya* (The Shadow of a Gun, 2011) have been published to date. Most of the stories of his second collection are set amidst the political turmoil in Nepal. An editor of *Antarbodh,* a tri-monthly literary magazine, Bastola is associated with the literary organizations Nepali Literature Journalists' Organization, Progressive Writers' Organization, and *Janasahitya Manch Nepal.*

Homshankar locates the evils of society in his stories and the voice of subjugated classes is apparent in them. Of his story writing, Modnath Prashrit remarks that Homshankar offers a "microscopic observation on evil" in his stories. The present story, *Bandukko Chhaya,* from his second collection, draws a grim picture of a farmer (a conflict victim) by means of a friendly conversation between two people. The writer supports peace by advocating a "nonviolent movement." These lines are noteworthy: "The meaning of revolution is not only to carry guns. It is also to carry rationales. The nonviolent movement spearheaded by Mahatma Gandhi was also a revolution."

The Shadow of a Gun

He was the rebel, who had fought many wars. He was a war veteran capable of handling all the consequences of the battlefield. He had heard the harsh voices and frantic cries of injured fighters. He had seen their miserable conditions while they were dying on battlefield begging for life. His friends, taking bullets and bombs, had died in front of him. However, he continued to encourage his fellow fighters to bravely fight the enemy.

Though many of his plans were successful, his plan for defeating a camp of enemies had been insurmountable for him and his fellow soldiers. They had attempted to attack the camp as many as four times. The camp was at the top of a hill, and below the hill was a low area with a riverbank. Human settlements and government offices were on the riverbank. It was difficult for the rebels to reach the camp and fight.

At a distance there was a beautiful mountain. The soul of the sentry would echo with a rushing sound from the river below the hill. The sentry and his comrades were aware of any sound coming through the still night.

Thus the soldiers had passed several nights. They would realize that they were surviving only after they had heard a rooster's crow in the morning from a distant village.

The rebel wanted to enter the enemies' camp to gather their secret information. Neither his journey up to the camp nor his objective of stealing the information was easy. There were checkpoints at many places. He would be arrested and killed instantly if his plans were discovered. Despite this risk, he made a bold decision, and putting himself in danger, he passed the police checkpoints and hurried towards the camp. He was in the guise of an ordinary man. The police let him go from each checkpoint thinking that he was only a villager.

The rebel had had many war-related experiences. One of them was his long experience with underground life. After his involvement in the war, he learned to carry a gun, though before it he had only known how to take his goats to graze and how to hurl stones or sticks to drive them back to their pen in his village. He would make gunpowder and explosives from water pipes. He planted bombs in many places under his party's direction. Once his heart was broken in one of the explosions he had caused.

****

In the explosion of a landmine the rebel had set off, one Dhane Mailo was killed on the scene while he was plowing a field. Though the death of the pair of oxen had little effect on him, he was shocked at Dhane's death.

Dhane was a village pauper. He lived in a hut. His oven used to get muddy when water leaked from his roof during the rainy season. He was the last surviving member of his family. His wife had died last year when a landslide in Barbote buried her while she was returning home from a field. That is why Dhane's death had hurt the rebel deeply.

When Dandaghare Mahajan, an eminent person of the village, had died two months prior to the death of Dhane's wife, the whole village had descended to the riverbank to pay a last tribute; but no more than twenty people attended Dhane's wife's funeral. He heard that the administration had given the landslide victims a little compensation after they had gone to the district headquarters. Dhane, however, did not get any aid because he could not manage the transport fare to go to the headquarters. Thus, he was deprived of disaster relief, too.

One day Dhane was returning home after plowing his landowner's field when he met the rebel. "When did you return from town, Son? I heard that you have gone to join the revolution. Is it true the revolution is for poor people like us?" he had asked.

"Yes, you're right, brother. We're fighting against the landowning exploiters. But we need the support of people like you," thus the rebel had asked for Dhane's support.

"We cannot manage even one square meal a day unless we plow other's fields. The life of poor people like us hangs on a plow and spade." Dhane had said, mopping the sweat from his forehead. He then climbed up the hill placing his plow on his shoulder.

The rebel had felt pity for him seeing him dressed in rags.

A few days later hearing the news of Dhane's death, the rebel's heart had broken a little. "Why are the poor and underdogs of society targeted if we are fighting for them? It's a shame! Killing innocent people is our mistake. We should apologize to the innocent mothers, children, and elderly people who are victimized by the war, and to the relatives of the many citizens who have been killed. Otherwise, history will curse us," the rebel had thought.

****

He was now an underground rebel and his records had already been circulated to all police posts. When he was forced to go underground, he was known by his pseudonym. The police had issued a warrant for his arrest on the basis of his photo and the pseudonym, but they were unsuccessful as they were unable to find out his real name. The police had gotten only a little information about him. His name was on the list of wanted suspects that was conveyed to security camps and police posts. But, on that day, the rebel crossed the police posts with his tricks and finally reached the army camp.

The rebel was walking around in front of the camp and was

taken aback when he ran into a robust man in combat dress with different insignias on his shoulder.

"Hello, Friend! Where are you going? We haven't seen each other for a long time, huh?" asked the man. The rebel was surprised at the sudden meeting, and he shook hands with his old friend.

"Ah, I'm heading to the village over there to meet my relatives," the rebel said quickly so that his old friend would not have a chance to doubt him.

The man had been the rebel's closest classmate while they were studying together. At that time, the rebel had helped the man in his studies, as the rebel was relatively smarter. The man requested the rebel to stay with him that night. "Friend, what are you doing these days? Let's stay together today. It has been a long time since we met." No sooner had the words of request slipped from the major's mouth than the rebel knew that his friend was the chief of the camp. It was like receiving an unexpected and beneficial gift.

"Of course, we are meeting after a long time. I had many times tried to meet you but was unable. I had heard that you were promoted to a major, but I did not even get time to congratulate you. Thank God we met today. It seems that God has arranged our meeting at the right time," the rebel spoke hyperbolically to win his friend's affection.

The rebel's intention was to enter the camp as the major's trusted guest. He wanted to be as close as he had been in their student life. He said that he was happy to meet his friend. Because it was a happy occasion, the major ordered sumptuous food and drinks. Though the rebel was not inured to drinking, he drank a little when he couldn't turn down his friend's offer. He pretended that he was drunk. The major explained the details of the camp's activities to his friend. The rebel secretly noted the information about the camp's security and its drawbacks. The rebel requested to observe the camp. The major, falling under his insistence, gave him a tour. The major received salutes from soldiers wherever they went in the camp. The rebel asked the major about the possible attack of enemies and the camp's weaknesses while the major briefed all to him as a confidant.

The rebel had already said that he was a government employee. The major believed this and explained to him the army's war tactics, methods of defense, and on the top of that he revealed their plans to fight the rebels. He added that each soldier was ready to fight off possible night attacks. He also said that each officer and soldier had been passing the nights living their lives on the edge of a knife. The rebel listened as the major explained. When the major expressed his opinion about the rebels, the rebel became furious inside despite nodding his head in agreement.

"It is rumored that the security personnel have even been troubling people without apparent reason. The rebel's claim that they have been fighting for the people," he spewed venom against his rivals. "Why are they fighting, Friend? They say they're fighting for the poor people, but they bomb the people who do not even get to fill their belly halfway. They do not hesitate to kill a plowman and oxen in the field. The rich and the exploiters of villages are in the headquarters for their safety, but we are passing the nights putting our lives on knife's edge for them. A farmer in the village was killed by a bomb while he was plowing a field a few days ago. Tell me, what was his crime? What had he done to the rebels? He was only a plowman for his landowner. His home was in such a dilapidated condition that it was not suitable even for a cowshed. What kind of People's War is this?"

The rebel remembered Dhane while the major said this. He was silent.

"Friend, you live in town. Perhaps you don't know the real

suffering experienced by the people living in villages. We might also have tortured them. I don't say we haven't done wrong. Of course many citizens have been arrested and killed on the charge of supporting or cooperating with the rebels during the war. Yes, both the innocent and the guilty might have been victims, but what about the trouble the rebels cause to innocent people? Yes, we, too, don't like war, nor do we like bearing enmity for the rebels, despite the fact that we have to follow the government's orders. We are fighting with our own brothers; one Nepali is fighting with another. Why are we fighting? Tell me! What do we get from the war? We get only suffering, grief, destruction, poverty, uncertainty, and ugliness? The beautiful and peaceful country of yesterday is burnt in the fire of war. Whether we win or lose, we will be neither winners nor losers. The people ruling from the center win.

"We pass several sleepless nights on the battlefield with guns as our pillows. Why don't the rebels understand this? When has power ever been gotten with the force of a gun? If they are fighting for people, first they have to win people's hearts. They are daydreaming if they think that they can win the war with guns. If they want to come to the helm of the government, why don't they come through elections? Our duty is to follow the government's order. They can order us after joining the government, and we will have to follow them as well. Fighting amongst ourselves, we achieve nothing but the death of one Nepali by another." He vented his anger against the destructive rage of the war and the deaths of his friends and brothers and innocent citizens.

The rebel listened silently as the major spoke. With the deepening night, the major asked him to go to bed on the condition that they would continue to talk the next day.

Lying in bed, the rebel started to ponder. "Why are we fighting? What do we get by killing innocent people and government soldiers who carry guns to fill their bellies and those of their family? The tears and suffering of their families are an unbearable burden for the country. This is what we get from the war. The meaning of revolution is not only to carry guns. It is also to carry rationales. The nonviolent movement spearheaded by Mahatma Gandhi was also a revolution. The same revolution restored freedom in India. But why are we still mad for the power of guns? Why don't we try to get in the government by asking for votes from the people? Why? One person's vote is equal to one bullet from a gun. How much more power a vote has than a bullet! How powerful is the American president, who is chosen through an election!" He thought further, "Now we must change at all costs. We should ask for an election with the present government. We should go to the polls and win the people's hearts first. I wish an elected government could be powerful and able to make decisions even in tough times."

He raised his hands and brought them close to his face and clutched them to each other. Then he lay on his bed and slept. He remembered his gun just before he fell asleep. Before he had set out for the enemies' camp, his hand had been holding the gun. He had fired the gun so many times with his hands, it was as if he had a hangover from it. He would think of himself as a fearsome person when he held the gun. He opened his hands and looked at them. He still saw the shadow of the gun. He rubbed his hands together and clapped them to clear the illusion. The shadow was still there. He woke up abruptly. It was morning. The rebel got up from his bed and stole away through the camp's gate without a parting word to his friend. He just left a message at the gate about his leaving and walked along the road. He hurried eastward. His silhouette slowly faded from the camp's gate.

*****

NIRMALACHARYA (1976)

Saugat Acharya writes under the pen name Nirmal Acharya. He was born in Ratapani of Pyuthan district, in western Nepal. He has served as a District Committee In-Charge (Dang) and as a member of the Tharuwan State Committee affiliated with the Unified Communist Party of Nepal-Maoist. In the course of his participation in student politics during the political unrest in Nepal, he was arrested in 1998, taken captive for two months, and sent to jail where he was imprisoned for thirty months. Acharya began writing literature since his forced disappearance and imprisonment. His poems, short stories, and memoirs are published in different literary journals and magazines. Eleven of his stories are collected in *Sankalpa Yatra* (A Resolute Journey, 2009), which includes the present story.

Moving incidents based on real life, and sharp-straightforward sentences are the arresting features in Acharya's stories. Dr. Gopindra Poudel observes: "After reading his [Nirmal Acharya's] stories, readers quest for the meaning of living. They attempt to evaluate life through the eyes of class struggle." The incident retold in the story *Euta Rastrasewakko Diary* (A Civil Servant's Diary) is based on a real event that Acharya heard while he was in jail. "The incident in the story was inspired by an event that actually took place in Dang," he says. This story portrays how civil servants were used to murder innocent people while the country was in the throes of revolutionary change. The first-person narrator of the story recalls a recent night's painful event when his commander shoots a pregnant woman for allegedly being a rebel's wife.

A Civil Servant's Diary

It is pouring relentlessly. Some of the days are so boring. It is the month of *Bhadra.* This is the time for crunching the roasted maize, but I have been following other's commands all throughout the days. Sometimes I feel frustrated. What an unlucky day it was when I took this job! Instead of being serious in my studies during my school days, what did I do? Now I am under someone else's command. Right now at home, Mother might be roasting the maize, sitting cross-legged on the kitchen floor. There was a severe drought this year, so the yield of the maize crop can't have been good. Still, the maize roasted by Mother is excellent! Ah! It is a great thing to have maize and whey, even if it is thinned with water. The taste of whey really begs description. What is the use of conjuring up memories of home while I am now in this situation?

I don't know where the hell we will be taken again today. Yesterday they marched us through the jungle saying that something really big would happen. Moreover, they made me an op, and I was overwhelmed with fear. Some went by the hotel—we call helicopters "hotels." We, the unlucky ones, went on our own two legs, a number-eleven vehicle. A path of dense jungle! We shrank with fear even at the sound of monkeys jumping from one branch to the other. Even the chirps of birds made our hearts skip a beat. Three hours! Yes, I had my op for exactly three hours. Oh! Days pass by, but God knows how they pass. I sometimes get frustrated; I feel like going to my mother at home and whining like a baby. But can I leave the job of my own accord? To get a job in those days was so difficult. I got it through my backdoor influence. How strange, now I can't leave the same job, no matter what I do. Alas! What days I face! Sometimes I feel like quitting the job and going across the border for one or two more years. But God knows what is keeping me. I run here and there all day and sleep for only a few hours at night. And do we get to sleep properly? Whistles! Firings! We are kept on red alert all twenty-four hours. Thank God this is the way my days pass, and I cannot drop the job all of a sudden. It's more like I don't have time to quit it and run away somewhere as a traitor.

Well, I was recounting the events of the day before yesterday. We were led on a march, having been told that something big would come to pass. They had us walk through the jungle. We did not hear a dickybird. The men of our team are very wild. Better not to call them *men*; they are butchers, skillful butchers. Whoever is met on the way is shot. Our duty starts at the crack of dawn and continues till four p.m. We have to return to our cage after four, otherwise a tiger could eat us if night falls in the jungle. Yes, it's true that our plight is no different from that of a goat. Enclosed in a cage, walked under the commander's order! The only difference is that a goat is a vegetarian. We eat meat, or rather, we drink blood — the red-hot blood of men. My head spins just thinking about it.

Ah! What laziness has gripped me? Where might we be taken again today? Wherever else we are taken, I pray that I don't have to face such an incident as the day before yesterday. My God, what a terrific sight that was! I am still not sure whether she was a criminal or not, but surely it was a tragic event.

It was hardly four in the morning. With a repeated cry— "A spy came, a spy came"—we were all rousted out of bed while we were still in deep sleep. The stupid commander jumps with joy whenever the chance to kill men comes along. But we are no different than he. For us, too, it's a good chance to open fire.

Twenty-five firing, seventy-five hiding! Then we sell the bullets to the storekeeper, a worthless fellow, who gives only fifteen rupees for one bullet. Any chance to open fire is good for us; we wildly fire the bullets even for the smallest of reasons. Once we open the fire, there is the chance to sell as many as one hundred to one hundred fifty bullets. The storekeeper buys them secretly, but who knows what he does with them. I guess he sells them for a profit. Ah! Who cares what he does with them! He gives us fifteen rupees for one bullet, and that's enough. Fifteen rupees can buy a plate of *momos*.

Yes, we were made to walk from four a.m. the day before yesterday. My God! What a roll call the devil commander of ours took! He said that a commander of notorious terrorists was hiding around. The rebel commander was to be killed in case he could not be arrested alive, he said, and went on and on. He kept me in the assault group. I don't know what has happened to me; he always keeps me as cannon fodder in the front line when the time for a possible confrontation comes. However, he keeps me at the back of the troop when there is no danger. I was scared to death while we picketed the house. Our hearts pounded with fear.

The house was, in fact, that of a poor Tharu family. Everything inside could easily be seen from outside. We lit a torch and looked in. We saw a pregnant woman with a toddler of about two in her lap. How quickly that there was going to be a second baby while the first baby was still in her lap! She was a real sex kitten. Fair complexioned. Shapely hands and legs. Her face was even more beautiful. But, for heaven's sake, no evil intentions were evoked in me at seeing her. Is she menstruating? Her skin seemed a little brownish grey, as if she had put powder on her round beautiful face. How could that be the powder? The poor thing might have suffered from anemia. I must admit that I was overcome with pity for her.

In no time the commander fell on her, kicking, and shouted, "Where? Where is the terrorist?"

Her husband is a terrorist? Anger surged somewhere in me as well. I lifted my leg to kick her, but I don't know what stopped me from doing so. I swear to God I had pity for the woman. She was sitting cross-legged with the child in her lap. She only stared at us with her unblinking eyes. We could not understand what she was uttering. She was probably saying, "I won't say. I won't say," in her Tharu language.

Her hair was pulled until it was disheveled, and then she was dragged. She was thrashed and pushed from one side to the other, but she remained tightlipped about her husband. Pushing a nine month pregnant woman from one wall to the other looked so funny. While she was jerked from behind, her bloated stomach went farther than the rest of her body, in the way a propulsive engine might pull a man forward. We took great pleasure pushing her from this side to that for a while. She began to breathe loudly like the running bellows of a blacksmith, but did not speak a word.

Meanwhile, my eyes were fixed on a hencoop while the commander was grilling her. There were six eggs. I broke them one by one and finished them in six gulps. Then I put the eggshells in the hencoop. I felt as though I got a little more energy. The woman was now standing with her baby tightly pressed to her chest. She did not cry or speak a word. "Come on, why don't you tell us, you fucker?" The commander began to yank her hair again. "Take this, sinner." Oh, what a fearless woman: she spat in the commander's face. I swear I had never seen such a woman in my life. I was furious but could not kick her. I don't know what I was thinking at the time! I thought if I kicked her she would have died for no apparent reason. Yes, it's absolutely true: she seemed the type of beautiful woman whose death would have haunted me forever.

How soon that commander from hell became infuriated; he tortured the poor thing in her pathetic condition. He became livid with anger simply because she had spat on his face. "Son of a bitch, shoot her," he shouted at me. To shoot her, or not to shoot her? I was in a dilemma. Yes, I would have to shoot her because it was the commander's order, but I could not. I swear to God I did not know what happened to me! And, again, why should that motherfucker give the order to me alone? He had already gotten me to kill seventeen people with these hands. That woman would have been the eighteenth. I used to feel a great pleasure while shooting at men's chests. But that day I could not shoot her. I don't know what happened to me; I could not pull the trigger.

The commander jumped on me and seized my weapon before I could say Jack Robinson. He looked as mad as a hornet. I swear I had never seen such anger manifested even on the face of Rate. I could only gawk at him. He opened fire in the flash of a second. He shot at her womb. The poor woman's abdomen was exposed, gurgling. I could not bear to see the ghastly scene. I swear to God, I felt so much pity for her. A fetus fell from the poor thing's broken womb. How strange! The baby slowly slid through the embryonic fluid and onto the floor. Even the child that she had been holding in her hands fell with a thud. How can I describe the blood that was flooding out so terribly? So many things, so disgusting. What to say? Her intestines were hanging from her abdomen. Then, after a moment, the woman also collapsed. The two-year-old child was lying on the floor, silent and helpless. He spoke nothing, did not weep or cry but only breathed hard. I thought the fetus was also breathing in short pants. *'Will the baby be alive after coming out of a womb in such a way?'* I wondered.

What a funny curiosity came to me at the moment: I wanted to know whether the baby was a boy or a girl. Well, I am recounting the event. When I slightly turned the child with a thin shred of cloth, I knew it was a girl. The mother was dead and the daughter as well while the two-year-old child was weltered in a pool of blood. I felt so much pity. What could I do even if I had pity for her? After all, her husband was a terrorist.

The rain outside is pouring nicely. I hope I will sleep more today. A command to go somewhere might come again. What kind of job did I take where I can't sleep fully even when I don't have energy to go to work? God! Sometimes I feel frustrated thinking that I took this job for nothing.

*****

SARALSAHAYATRIPOUDEL (1981)

Saral Sahayatri Poudel, born in Sindhupalchok district to the north-east of Kathmandu, is a promising young writer of short stories, memoirs, and poems. He is the brigade commander of the People's Liberation Army (PLA), affiliated with the UCPN-Maoist. Sahayatri's eighteen stories related to Nepal's Maoist-Government war are collected in *Krantika Kathaharu* (The Stories of Revolution, 2007). *Chhapamarko Geet* (Song of a Guerilla, 2010) is his collection of fifty-two poems. The poems are dedicated to the revolutionary fighters who were killed during the war. His own brother and sister were killed in the war.

Sahayatri's stories are rich with the sensitivity of feeling, vividity of presentation, simplicity of style, and compactness of expression. His stories raise the voice of subjugated classes and in them he offers soldier's viewpoints. Dr. Jagadishchandra Bhandari observes that his stories "are related to the People's War and the new realities that emerged after the war."

The present story titled *Hami, Dui Sipahi* (We, Two Soldiers) is a PLA soldier's nostalgic monologue. "I take a leaf out of the book of the battlefield of class struggle and verbalize my suffocated feelings into stories," Sahayatri says. The story's first person narrator, seeing his friend posted on duty for the national army, recalls painful experiences they both had in their village. The two opposing soldiers cannot verbalize their feelings due to their rivalry.

We, Two Soldiers

He is in combat dress this time as well. Standing upright, he is gripping his rifle. No more than the lower half of his body can be seen as it is sunk into the bunker. However, I easily knew him from a distance—my old friend Ajaya! I peered at him to know whether I was having an illusion, but it was Ajaya. Our families had given us similar names—Ajaya and Bijaya—probably because of our intimacy since childhood. My happiness knows no bounds seeing him suddenly today. I cannot talk with him because he is on duty. He, too, might have seen me! I notice him smiling from a distance.

The gun, the combat uniform he wears, and the heavy bag filled with bullets—seeing all, I conclude that they are his ornaments, his life, and, moreover, the means for his death. I am also on duty. I am a soldier for the People's Liberation Army. I also have a weapon—a small Mauser. I have hidden it inside my clothing as I am hardnosed in following the party policy of not showing one's weapon. I do not wear combat dress; only a blue safari uniform identifies us.

Both of us know that poverty is still the same in our homes, or rather, in our village. We can eat no other grains except *dhindo*. Once we buy a pair of clothes, we cannot buy another for years. The bodies of our families crawl with lice because we cannot use bathing soap, and most people in our village do not even know what soap is! The elites living in the city might think it a joke, wondering whether such a society still exists. But we two soldiers, victims of the same painful poverty, are close today, whereas yesterday we used to fight.

I still have vivid memories. Ajaya was a small boy and I was too. His younger sister turned to skin and bones after catching a fever. Jaundice made her so gaunt that she was no more than a blade of straw. His mother knocked on the doors of many neighbors asking for money for his sister's treatment, but all her efforts ended in vain. She was beaten when she went to ask for money from a rich man for whom she worked.

Finally the bed-ridden girl died without treatment. Ajaya wept bitterly, throwing himself into my embrace. Two days after his sister's death, he left the village without anyone's notice. "Look, Bijaya. I could not save my sister because of poverty. She loved me so much. Now I must go to the city to earn money," he said to me one day before he left the village. I was helpless. I did not stop him. Later I came to know that he had enlisted in the government army.

I stayed in the village for a few more weeks. People had started to talk under their breath. "It is known that the Maoists killed *jethamukhiya* of the neighboring village. It is rumored that they have also written letters to his two brothers and the party is likely to take similar action against them in case they don't return the villager's *tamasuk* and land ownership certificate."

Such secret talks and gossip rippled throughout. After a few days it was learnt that in the neighboring village the police had killed two Maoists in cold blood, stabbing them with a bayonet. I also saw the ghastly bodies. The police brandished guns and had us carry the bodies up to the bazaar.

A number of unanswered questions kept on running in my innocent mind: "Ultimately what had they done except threaten the exploiter *mukhiya*? I learned that the villagers had celebrated his death by putting out their *tuki* lamps for many days. For the first time, the villagers learned that others greater than him also lived in society. Out of prejudice the police killed those who had fought for the Nepali people. What did the police get at last? The men could have been arrested and punished according to the law if they had done wrong! Is it Nepali law to punish the murderer with a murder?" I had never heard about such a law. It occurred to me that the police were people's enemies.

In a few days there was another rumor in the village: "Gange, of the CPN-UML, finked on the Maoists, and the Maoists beheaded him, too."

"The Maoists did right if this is true!" the words suddenly slipped from my mouth while we were chatting in the tea shop.

"Hey, hold your tongue. You may die! Who are the terrorists you speak of anyway?" a so-called communist—a worthless fellow—exploded, so loudly that our ears burned.

"The God of the poor!" I snapped while he was still venting his anger on me. "You are the devil's brothers! Why do you boast? Villagers have felt relief after the death of that hypocrite *mukhiya*. Gange spied on the two poor men who were killed later. Was that right?" I have a hot temper, so I spoke with no self-control.

"Son of a bitch! What proof do you have to call Gange a spy?" he countered bellicosely. A tense situation had already begun. He was angry and I was double that.

"Was his corpse not proof? Do Maoists go chopping people up without a reason?"

He could not stand my belligerence and left the tea shop, warning, "I know now! Wait and see. I will show you who I am."

Having heard all this at home, mother scolded me severely. "Why in God's name do you have to be over smart? Aren't there other men smarter than you? What is wrong with having a little self-control? You will be killed soon." Mother started sobbing.

"They will kill you. They won't leave you alive. Leave home to save your life!"

That night I went to sleep at Sete's house in the next village, fearing for my safety at home. My inclination proved right when I learned that police raided our home that night. I came to know that the police had dragged my mother out and beaten her after they did not find me. Then they went back threatening her life.

My little brother came to me early in the morning and said, "Brother, don't come home. They won't leave you alive."

From there I fled to the jungle. I had no other option. Where to go? What to eat? I was without plans. I had only ten rupees in my pocket. Ultimately, what would be the use of money even if I had more? During the first ten days of hardships, I overcame fear, fright, and terror for the first time in my life.

I used to think that the Maoists lived in the jungle, ate wild roots, rhizome, and yams, and fought for the people's liberation. One day I was contacted by them through a shepherd and felt proud. I was surprised when I came to know that the Maoists live not in the jungle but in the hearts of people.

We undertook an extremely horrible journey of sacrifice after that. I was deployed as a soldier of the People's Army a few days after joining the party. As time passed, we continued to develop the party formation regularly.

One night we attacked the army camp that had intruded our base camp. We continuously marched ahead, bravely sacrificing ourselves and using the dead bodies as shields against the enemy's attack. I was a novice at fighting. The earth under our feet was soaked with blood. Dozens of friends embraced their heroic death, but we never left the entrenchment. We continuously moved ahead even though it meant stepping over the dead bodies.

My close friend, who had been beside me, was shot. He had been caught in the enemy's fire and he screamed with pain. The enemies showered him with more bullets. He was very far from us. Maoist slogans came from his mouth. He did not yield to his enemies and did not stop shouting "Long live . . ." and "Down with . . ." no matter how many bullets rained on him. Replete with a sense of revenge, we waited for an opportunity to move forward.

When the enemies were tired of firing on us, my friend's wife—God knows where had she been—walked ahead without shrinking from the fierce confrontation. She picked up her beloved's gun. He had perhaps another breath and might have wanted to say farewell to his wife, but she proceeded indifferently and attacked the enemies' main bunker. Finally she took command of it. Unfortunately, a bullet from an unseen corner pierced her chest. Overcome with pain, she tottered over to her beloved and fell on his chest before breathing her last. Altogether we started our offense from all sides. We marched ahead. The surviving stragglers surrendered. Some died while the remaining mangled or maimed struggled with the death.

Passing through the enemies' painful cries inside the camp and crying myself, too, I ran ahead. Then I heard the yells of an injured person who was calling my name, "Bijaya . . . Bijaya . . ." It was a familiar voice I had heard somewhere before. I thought it was perhaps a fallen friend calling from somewhere. I stopped and peered with a torch. "Bijaya . . . Bi-je," he spelled my name with difficulty. The face covered in blood was unrecognizable. He was unable to support himself because both his legs were fractured. I went closer to him. The injured person was faced down. "Who are you?" I asked, laying him supine on the ground.

He smiled and made a painful grimace. "D-do you not know me? You have been smart, huh! All right! I . . . I am Ajaya, your childhood friend. Now . . . now your enemy!" I could only stare at him as he said this gasping for breath. He tried to speak again but could not. I caught his hands and rested his head on my lap. Recalling our childhood days, tears welled up in my eyes, but I could not let the tears flow. Nor could I embrace him. "My brother! My friend! How come you are here in such a condition?" I murmured with emotion.

The ground where he was lying was wet with blood. He suddenly slipped from my lap and, turning towards me, spoke, "Bije, I'm going to ask two things . . . Will you do them?"

I was looking at him silently. Perhaps he thought I was consenting and went on, "Bijaya . . . Do not tell of my . . . my painful death . . . to my mother. Otherwise she . . . will cry . . . for my . . . pain. But do inform her of my death because otherwise the authorities might hide the news of my death. The next thing I ask you is . . . and you can do it surely enough . . ." His voice trailed off for a moment. What might he ask? The question arose in me amidst that tragic moment.

Again he began to speak, "Bijaya! I called you here . . . not to ask . . . you to save my life but . . . but to ask you to give me peace in my death. This time . . . my wound is severe . . . I am suffering an . . . an intolerable pain. My friend! Dear brother! If you really are kind to me, please, shoot me! My pain . . . will be relieved if you do this for me. My brother . . . have mercy u-upon me and shoot me with y-your gun. Please . . . do this for me."

I was highly emotional. However, controlling myself, I immediately called a medical team and asked them to give him an injection and saline water. Then he must have passed out. Giving medication to all the wounded soldiers and covering them with any available blankets, we headed towards our destination.

****

Today we meet in the peace rally for the second time after ten years. His legs might have been cured. Holding his gun, he is on duty on a red alert. Perhaps he wants to talk with me. He might be eager to share his story since we parted. Unfortunately, he has an order from above, "Don't communicate with any of the Maoist cadres. The Maoists again want to invite war and plant the seeds of conflict among our soldiers!" and so on and so forth.

Blinking his eyes, he is looking at me from the bunker. I am also looking at him. I am walking around the road with the small Mauser. Holding the gun's muzzle, he is on standby in the bunker. I know what his eyes are saying: "Bijaya, please make me like you so that I can walk freely on the road." I am also saying silently, "Ajaya! Why can't you break the chain? Why must you stay like a captive forever?" Whatever we exchanged in feelings, ultimately we both want peace and freedom. Not a dead peace, we want a changed fresh morning. We want to change the history and the future. But his Generals do not let us meet; they confine his reasoning. Perhaps they hope for another war because they do not have to fight. They do not have to be killed. They get more income by waging war than by making peace. The people who die from the war turn out to be poor people like Ajaya, who have to follow their superior's orders. These warmongers do not care about the death of poor people. Therefore, we two soldiers have same wishes: change and peace.

*****

About the Compiler & Editor

A Master's Degree in English Literature from Tribhuwan University in Nepal, Ram C. Khatri compiled, translated, and edited short stories and novels. His works include *Rebel* (2011), a collection of short stories into English; *Rupantaran* (2008), a Nepali language version of Franz Kafka's The Metamorphosis; and *Bishwaka Utkrista Aadhunik Kathaharu* (2007), some American and European short stories into Nepali. Mr. Khatri also edited *Vidrohi* (2011), a Nepali language version of *Rebel* and *After the Sunset* (2012), a collection of English short stories by Bhagirathi Shrestha, a popular Nepali writer. *Abraham Lincoln Ko Katha* (2012), Ram wrote in Nepali, is for school children. He lives in New York, studying publishing at Pace University.

Glossary

Achheta - Mixture of rice grains and vermillion powder used for worshiping.

Astami - The eighth day of Dashain on which animals are sacrificed.

Bhadra - A month of the rainy season, equivalent to August-September.

Bindi - A kind of traditional cigarette with a twist of tobacco rolled inside a leaf.

Chaitra - The last month in the Nepalese calendar, beginning in mid-March.

Chautari - A raised platform shaded by banyan tree built for the purpose of resting and talking.

Danphe - National bird of Nepal.

Deurali - A small passage at the mountain top.

Dhiki - Wooden machine for husking rice.

Dhindo - Millet powder paste, food for the poor.

Dhurseli - A narrow leafed bush

Ghorahi - The headquarters of Dang.

Ghodruk - Dried green vegetable.

Handi - A flat-bottomed earthen pot.

Haruwacharuwas - Domestic helpers who plow fields and graze cattle.

Janto - Stone grinder.

Jaulo - Boiled soft rice porridge.

Jethamukhiya - Oldest headman.

Khurpa - A large sickle.

LTTE - The separatist organization the Liberation Tigers of Tamil Eelam, which fought for a separate Tamil state in Sri Lanka.

Liwang - The headquarters of Rolpa district where the Maoist war began in Nepal.

Lungi - A kind of sarong.

Pirka - A flat piece of wood to sit on.

Rate - A comedian in the Nepali film Chino.

Roti - Bread made from stoneground wholemeal flour.

Sindoor - A traditional red powder usually worn by married Hindu women along the parting of their hair.

Swastishanti - Benedictory incantation to drive away evil spirits.

Tamasuk - A written agreement for the ownership of land.

Tilhari - Jewelry of married Hindu women.

Yogi - Ascetic.